P9-DYD-573

Cosmic

ALSO BY

FRANK COTTRELL BOYCE

Millions

Framed

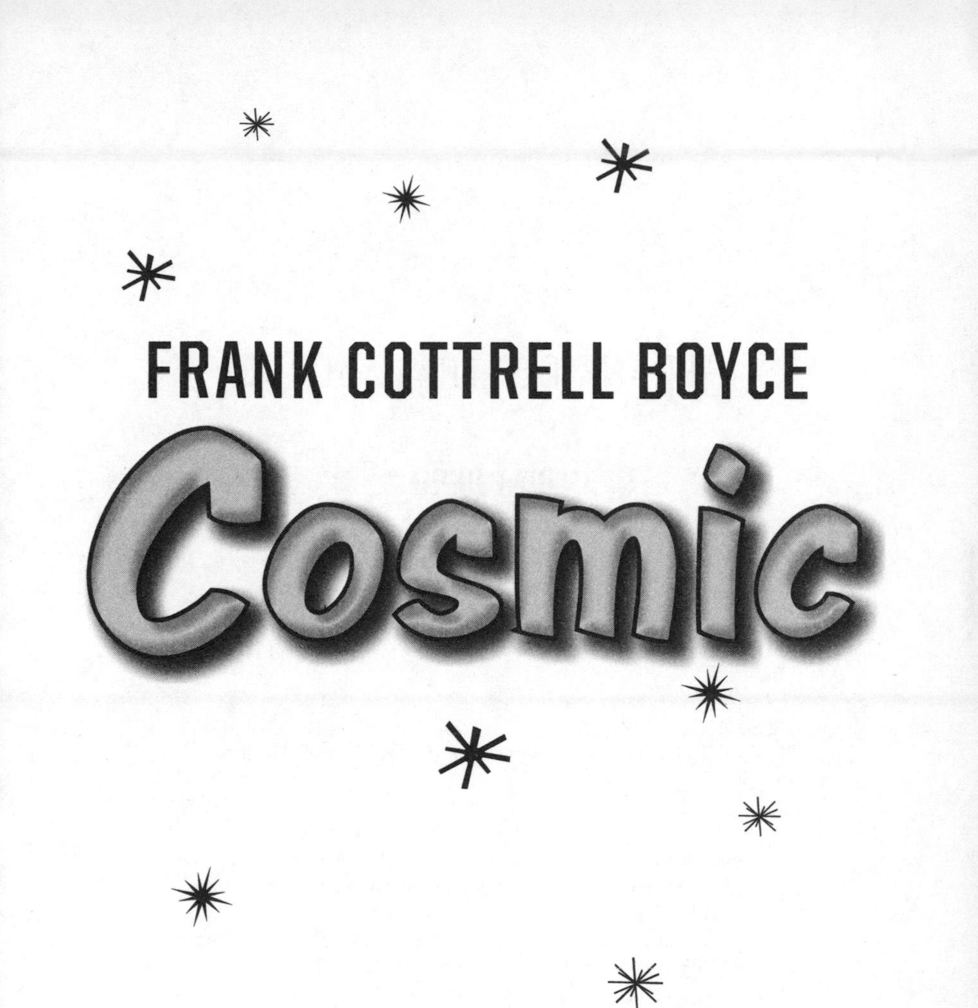

WALDEN POND PRESS
An Imprint of HarperCollins*Publishers*

To my parents—
a book about the magic of parents

Walden Pond Press is an imprint of HarperCollins Publishers.

Cosmic
Copyright © 2008 by Frank Cottrell Boyce
All rights reserved. Printed in the United States of America.
No part of this book may be used or reproduced in any manner whatsoever without written permission except in the case of brief quotations embodied in critical articles and reviews. For information address HarperCollins Children's Books, a division of HarperCollins Publishers, 10 East 53rd Street, New York, NY 10022.
www.harpercollinschildrens.com

Library of Congress catalog card number: 2009927741

ISBN 978-0-06-183683-1 (trade bdg.)
ISBN 978-0-06-183686-2 (lib. bdg.)

Typography by Andrea Vandergrift
10 11 12 13 14 CG/RRDB 10 9 8 7 6 5 4 3 2 1
❖
First American Edition, 2010
Originally published in Great Britain
by Macmillan Children's Books in 2008

@latestnews: A rocket, launched yesterday from a private site in northern **China**, is missing. Yesterday the Internet was alive with rumors of a secret manned space mission. Today **NASA** and the **Russian Federal Space Agency** both confirmed that a rocket did take off but denied it was theirs. The rocket entered high orbit and then disappeared into deep space. No manned rocket has left Earth's orbit since ***Apollo 17*** in 1972.

Posted four hours ago from web

I Am Not Exactly in the Lake District

Mom, Dad—if you're listening—you know I said I was going to the South Lakeland Outdoor Activity Center with the school?

To be completely honest, I'm not exactly in the Lake District.

To be completely honest, I'm more sort of in space.

I'm on this rocket, the *Infinite Possibility*. I'm about two hundred thousand miles above the surface of the Earth. I'm all right . . . ish.

I know I've got some explaining to do. This is me doing it.

I lied about my age.

I sort of gave the impression I was about thirty. Obviously I'm more sort of thirteen-ish. On my next birthday.

To be fair, everyone lies about their age. Adults pretend to be younger. Teenagers pretend to be older. Children wish they were grown-ups. Grown-ups wish they were children.

It's not like I had to try very hard, is it? Everyone always thinks I'm older than I really am, just because I'm tall. In St. Joan of Arc Primary the teachers seemed to think that height and age were the same thing. If you were taller than someone, you must be older than them. If you were tall and you made a mistake—even if it was only your first day—you got, "You should know better, big lad like you."

Why, by the way? Why should a big lad know better just because he's big? King Kong's a big lad. Would *he* know the way to the bathroom on his first day at school? When no one had told him? No, I don't think he would.

Anyway, a few hours back the *Infinite Possibility* was supposed to complete a routine maneuver and basically it didn't. It rolled out of orbit, wrecking all the communications equipment, and now I'm very lost in space.

I've brought this mobile phone with me—because it's got pictures of home on it. It's also got an audio-diary function. That's what I'm talking into now. Talking makes me feel less lonely. Unless you get this message you won't know about any of this because this is a secret mission. They said that if it goes wrong they're going to deny all knowledge of it. And us. There's five of us on board. The others are all asleep.

Can you believe that, by the way? We're in a rocket,

spinning hopelessly out of control and into Forever, and what is their chosen course of action?

A nap.

When we got the maneuver just slightly wrong—just slightly enough to make us completely doomed—they all screamed for about an hour and then they dozed off.

I can't sleep. I can't get comfortable in sleeping bags because they're always too small for me.

Plus I think if I stay awake I might have an idea. And save us all. That's why I'm recording this on my Draxphone. If I do get home, I'm going to give it to you and then you'll understand how I ended up in deep space when I said I was going pond dipping in the Lake District.

If you are listening to this though, and you are not my mom and dad, you are probably a pointy-headed, ninety-legged, sucker-footed alien, in which case, can I just say, "Hello, I come in peace. And, if you happen to have the technology, please post this phone to:

Mr. and Mrs. Digby—23 Glenarm Close, Bootle, Liverpool 22, England, The Earth, Solar System, Milky Way, et cetera. If it's not too much trouble."

Completely Doomed

The slightly worrying thing is that I am sort of enjoying this. Being doomed is Not Good. But being weightless is Outstanding. Every time I lean forward I do a perfect somersault. When I stretch my arms in the air I levitate. Back on Earth my only special skills are being above average in math and height. Up here I've got so many skills I'm practically a Power Ranger.

Then there's the stars.

On Earth, our house is right next to the New Strand Shopping Center. The multistory parking lot blots out most of the sky. The only stars I ever really noticed were the ones on the "It's Your Solar System" glow-in-the-dark mobile I got when I was nine. And the only reason I noticed them was that they kept getting tangled in my hair. Mobiles do not make good presents for persons of above average height.

The stars look different from here. There's a lot more of them, for one thing. Big swirls and knots and clouds of them, so bright they hurt to look at. When you're in it, space looks like the biggest firework display ever—except it's on pause. It looks like freeze-frame fireworks. Even if you're Completely Doomed, you've got to be impressed.

The only bad thing about the view is that it doesn't include Earth. We haven't seen it since we rolled out of orbit. I said to the others, "Well, it must be somewhere. We're probably just facing the wrong way. We'll find it. Definitely." But that didn't seem to calm them down. One of them—Samson Two—drew me a diagram to prove that even if we were facing the wrong way we should still be able to see it. I said, "So what are you saying? That we've fallen into some magic wormhole and come out on the other side of the universe?"

"Possibly."

"That the whole Earth just vanished? That it's gone?"

"Possibly."

They all screamed until they wore themselves out, and then they went to sleep.

At least sleep uses less oxygen.

I have tried to imagine that there's someone on the other end of this phone. Someone unusually quiet. I've also tried to make actual phone calls. I sort of thought the signal might be better up here, being nearer to the satellites. But it doesn't seem to work like that.

My Favorite Gravity

I don't think the world has vanished. But it is worrying not being able to see it. After all, Earth is where I keep all my stuff. Thinking about all my favorite bits—my mom, and my dad, my bedroom, my computer—makes me feel a bit calmer. There's my massive Playmobil Viking ship that takes up half the floor. Or used to take up half the floor. I put it back in its box the day I discovered I'd grown facial hair. I just thought that anyone with a beard—even just a wispy one—is probably too old for Playmobil.

I say *I* discovered the facial hair. To be honest, I never noticed it, because we've got energy-saving lightbulbs in the bathroom. It was other people who pointed it out to me, during the Year Six graduation trip to Enchantment Land.

The most famous ride in Enchantment Land is the Cosmic. All the way there, on the bus, everyone kept on about how big it was and how scary. Everyone had a brother or a cousin who had been on it and Never Been the Same Again. In case you don't know, the Cosmic is a kind of metal cage with two seats in. It's attached to the top of a massive crane by kind of big elastic bands. They pull the cage down to the ground with a chain and fasten it with an electromagnet. You sit inside and then they switch off the magnet. The elastic catapults you into the air and then snaps you back toward the ground again. Then you bounce up and down for a while. It's only frightening for about ten seconds, but for those ten seconds it is so frightening that Ben's cousin's hair supposedly turned completely white. And it goes so fast that Joe's next-door neighbor's stomach came loose and ended up stuck in his own neck and he had to have an operation. Apparently he'll show you the stitches if you ask him.

Despite these obvious drawbacks, everyone said they were going to go on it. Until we got there and discovered there was a height requirement—namely a wooden Martian holding his arm straight out and a speech bubble that said, "If you can walk under my arm, you can't take the Cosmic." Everyone could easily walk under the arm. Except me. It only came up to my shoulder. "Okay," said the man. "You're on."

See what I mean about height versus age? It's a height requirement, not an age requirement. Everyone was moaning, saying it wasn't fair and saying how rubbish it was being a kid and how they wished they were grown-ups. That's what they said. In fact, they were all blatantly relieved that they weren't tall enough.

The man said, "You'll need someone to go on with you. It's two at a time or no ride."

I looked at Mrs. Hayes, our teacher. She shrugged. "Are you allowed on if you're pregnant?"

"No," said the man, but you could hardly hear him because everyone was so excited by the news that Mrs. Hayes was having a baby.

"No one else?" said the man.

And everyone looked at the responsible parent who had very kindly accompanied our group—namely, my dad. He always comes on these things because he's a taxi driver, so he can choose what hours he works.

Florida Kirby kept nudging him, "Go on, Mr. Digby. Go on. My dad'd do it if he was here. My dad's dead brave." She more or less shoved him past the Martian and up the ramp. The man waved us into the cage and fastened us both in. I remember Dad saying, "Has anyone ever died on this?"

And the man glared at him. "No," he said. "No one has EVER died on my ride."

"Only asking," said Dad.

Then the man shut the door of the cage, looked at us through the bars and said, "But there's always a first time."

If we'd said, "Let me out!" then, it wouldn't have done any good because straightaway this incredibly loud music started up and dry-ice fog came pouring into the cage and lights were bouncing around us. They really believed in a big build-up. Dad gripped my hand and shouted, "Don't be scared, Liam." Before I could say, "I'm not scared," something went BANG and we were rocketing through the air. There's a horrible crushing feeling, like a big fist squeezing you into a ball. Then at the top it just lets go of you and you feel lighter than air and not scared of anything at all, as though all the fear had been squeezed out of you. The second bounce was nearly as high as the first, but it wasn't even a bit frightening. We sat there, the two of us, laughing madly while we waited for the elastic to calm down. We bounced five more times.

When we got off I was tingling all over and everything around me looked sort of more in focus than usual. Everything was crisper and brighter. The boys were all hanging around the wooden Martian, shouting and yelling and cheering. The girls were still hanging round Mrs. Hayes asking her about the baby. I realized we'd only been up there about two minutes.

Florida Kirby said, "Are you going to be sick?"

"No."

"Julie Johnson was sick on the Ghost Train."

She seemed to think that if I knew this, I might agree to be sick, just to fit in. Florida Kirby is obsessed with two things—celebrities and being sick. Give her a sick celebrity and she's in heaven.

I said, "That. Was. Golden. Can we do it again?"

Dad said, "Not with me, you can't."

"But . . ."

"Liam, what you've just had was a once-in-a-lifetime experience. And now you've had it."

He went off to play on the Hook-a-Duck. Wayne Ogunsiji was with him, and the two of them got into this profound conversation about Liverpool's defense. Dad said they were weak at the back. Wayne said they were solid at the back but they couldn't really distribute properly. Every now and then I'd see the cage of the Cosmic shoot up over the tops of the other rides, twisting and turning like a moon shot from a cannon, and part of me thought, I've done that. And the rest of me thought, I've got to do it again.

When it was time to leave, Mrs. Hayes marched us off to this special exit they've got just for school parties. I carried on watching for one last glimpse of the Cosmic.

I must've drifted a bit out of the line, because when I tried to walk through the gate the security man said, "Could you stand aside a moment, sir?" I stood aside and watched everyone else leaving.

When Dad went by he was so busy mentally managing

Liverpool's soccer team with Wayne Ogunsiji he didn't even glance at me. As soon as Dad'd gone through, the security guard closed the door and said to me, "The main exit's over there, mate. This is schoolkids only."

He thought I was a grown-up!

People always think I'm older than I am but no one had taken me for an actual grown-up before. I could've said, "I *am* a schoolkid. Please let me out," OR I could've said nothing, and seized the opportunity to have another go on the Cosmic. So I did have two options but somehow, in my head, they dwindled down to one.

I went straight back to the Cosmic.

The man in charge spotted me hanging around and said, "Didn't your mate like it?"

"My mate?" I realized he was talking about my dad.

"You know, you can do me a favor if you like. Help me plug the gaps."

"What gaps?"

"Well, I like to keep the ride busy. It doesn't look too tempting, the cage just standing there. A lot of people chicken out at the last minute. I like to have someone who can step in from time to time."

I said, "Sure," in a grown-up kind of voice and stood by the cage.

That afternoon I did the Cosmic with a boy whose mom was too scared to take him, a teenager who was doing it for a dare, someone whose girlfriend was too fat for the seat, and four others. Eight goes in all. The man said I must have a highly developed center of gravity. Every single time, I got the same Crispy New World feeling. It never wore off.

According to the man, the Cosmic generates 4 *g* on the way up. "That's four times the gravitational force exerted by the Earth—4 *g* is enough to make you appreciate how comfy normal gravity is. I used to have it set at 5 *g*, but people kept passing out, which wasn't good for business. You do have to feel sorry for anyone who lives on a high-gravity planet all the time. That must be really hard work."

Afterward the man bought some hot dogs and chips and we ate them in the cage, dangling gently from a piece of elastic high above the fair. You could see all the rides laid out like a model village, and sometimes a seagull went right past us. Finally, I spotted Dad walking quickly past the Fun House. I shouted, "Taxi!!!! Taxi!!!!" which usually works.

He looked everywhere but up. It was ages before he saw me.

I suppose if you're looking for me now, Dad, you're doing the same thing. Looking everywhere but up, in space. It was a laugh watching you then. But when we got back to the ground you weren't amused.

"Where the hell have you been? We counted you out of the exit. People swore they saw you on the bus. We were halfway to Bootle before we realized you weren't with us."

"I've been here. I was here the whole time. Wasn't I, mister?"

"Yeah," said the man in charge. "And what's your problem anyway, mate?"

"I'm not your mate. I'm his dad."

"You look a bit young to be his dad."

"He's twelve."

"What?"

"He's just unusually tall."

"It's not his height; it's his beard."

That was the first mention of the Premature Facial Hair.

And Dad said, "Liam. Bus."

Everyone cheered and clapped when I finally got on the bus. I sat by the window and tried to get a look at my new facial hair reflected in the glass. I could just make out little wisps of brown cotton candy. I said, "How did they get there? D'you think the extra gravity might have squeezed them out of my face?"

Randomly, this made Dad really furious. "Liam—blah blah—looking for you for the past two hours—blah blah. Had every taxi driver in the county looking for you. Reported your magical disappearance from a moving bus—"

"I wasn't on the bus."

"—your magical disappearance from a moving bus to the police."

"No!"

"And then I find you cheerfully waving and eating chips on a fairground ride. How d'you think I feel about that?"

"Happy that I'm alive?"

He glared at me and said, "Possibly. In some remote and noble corner of my heart, yes. But mostly no."

I said, "I'm sorry."

Then he said, "You should know better, a big lad like you."

That's the thing about parents. If you go missing, they worry that you might be dead. Then when they find you, they want to kill you.

Dad was furious because while he'd been worrying himself sick I hadn't been worried at all. Why wasn't I worried? Because I knew he'd come back for me. I never thought for a minute he wouldn't. When you're a kid you think your dad can do anything.

It's different now. If you ask me now if I think Dad is going to pop up at the controls of this rocket, two hundred thousand miles above the surface of the Earth, and fly us back to Bootle, I'd say probably not.

I suppose that means I'm not a kid anymore.

I Nearly Shaved Myself to Death

Even though I could barely see the Premature Facial Hair, once I knew it was there, I couldn't stop thinking about it. It was ticklish and it was tempting to stroke it. Stroking it made other people notice it and when other people noticed it they tended to shout, "Wolverine!" and worse. Which is why I decided to get rid of it.

I slashed at the brown cotton candy with Dad's razor, which did get rid of it. Sadly it also got rid of a lot of blood.

Sheets of blood just sort of fell out of my face. I wasn't quite sure what the procedure was so I squashed a towel into my chin, prayed that I wouldn't die and carried on squashing and praying for about an hour. I was starting to think that maybe I was already dead when Mom called me for supper. When I went down she said, "What happened to you? You look like you've boiled your face."

Dad said, "He's been shaving."

"What?" said Mom. "He can't shave! He's too young to shave! He's *much* too young to shave."

"Well, he's definitely too young to have a beard," said Dad. And he showed me how to shave in a less life-threatening manner.

"The only thing is," he said, "now you've started, you'll have to carry on. The hairs will get harder and harder the more you shave them."

So I don't get wisps of cotton candy anymore. I get this stuff that looks like naturally occurring toilet brush.

Mom said, "Liam, you've got to stop growing so fast. I'm not ready to lose my little boy yet."

Mom got so worked up about all this that she took me to see the doctor. The doctor said there was nothing to worry about. That made Mom really worried. She asked to see the specialist.

"Specialist in what?"

"Well, you read about these people, don't you, who grow up too fast? Their hair starts falling out when they're teenagers, then they get wrinkles and they look like old men but they're only twenty."

She'd never mentioned these people to me before. She must have noticed my look of absolute terror because she said, "They're very rare. But they do exist. You read about them on the Internet, don't you?"

I was relieved when the doctor said, "No, I don't think I have read about them, to be honest. I could send you to see a bone specialist at the children's hospital."

At the hospital they gave me scans, blood tests and an "I've been brave" sticker. They took me to see a specialist, then a special specialist. They both said that I was normal. Completely normal. Extra normal. Abnormally normal.

But tall.

"He's just a little boy," said Mom. "He's growing up too quickly."

"We all feel like that about our children, Mrs. Digby. The important thing is to remember that he is still a child. Even though he looks like a grown-up. Just because he can't shop in the children's clothes section anymore, that doesn't mean his childhood is over. Boys grow at different speeds. Particularly at this point in their lives. You might go back after the summer, Liam, and find that everyone's had a bit of a spurt and you're not even the tallest in the class."

"D'you know, that makes sense," said Mom. "His dad was tall at primary, and now look at him. He's well below average height."

"In fact," said Dad, "I'm slightly above average."

"In fact you are not."

"Only very slightly—but very, very definitely—I am above average."

"We'll talk about this another day," said Mom, which is what she always says when she wants you to shut up.

The special specialist was partly right about the growing spurts. Nearly everyone had one over the summer.

Including me.

When Mom wanted to mark my height on the "See How I Grow" chart in the kitchen, she had to get a chair to reach the top of my head. "Oh," she said, "you've had a spurt!"

And Dad said, "Seven inches is not a spurt. Seven inches is a mutation."

On my very first day at Waterloo High, I was the tallest person on the lower-school site.

The new uniform Mom had bought at the beginning of the summer didn't fit anymore and they had to send off for an extra-large lower-school blazer. I got a special dispensation to wear my own clothes for the first half-term.

When we went to get my travel pass for the bus to school, the woman in the office wouldn't believe I was school age so we had to go home and get my birth certificate. And then the next morning, when I showed it to the bus driver, she wouldn't believe it was mine, and I had to get off the bus and text Mom, and she came down and explained to the driver of the next bus that I was unusually tall for my age.

"It's not the height, love," said the driver. "It's the stubble."

Mom said, "Am I going to have to do this every morning?"

"Only till we all get used to him."

In the end, Mom sent off for a passport for me. I kept it in my pocket in case I got questioned again. Dad said, "That'll keep you out of trouble."

How wrong can a person be, by the way?

Dad also gave me his old mobile phone, so that if he ever lost me again—like in Enchantment Land—he would be able to find me. His phone's got DraxWorld on it. In case you don't know, that's this cosmic application that shows you your present location, directions to anywhere from anywhere, and also live satellite photographs of anything in the world. You can use it to look at volcanoes erupting. Tidal waves. Forest fires. Anything. Dad uses it to make sure the traffic is flowing smoothly on the bypass.

That first day at Waterloo High, I was on DraxWorld all the way to school on the 61 bus. I used it to look at theme parks and thrill rides. I found Oblivion in Alton Towers, Space Mountain in EuroDisney, the Knightmare in Camelot, Thunder Dolphin, Air . . . all of them. As the bus was crawling along Waterloo Road I typed in "Waterloo," wondering if I'd be able to get a satellite view of me on the bus. Instead the screen filled up with ten thousand options. There were Waterloos everywhere. Waterloo Station in London. Waterloo the port in Sierra Leone. Waterloo in Belgium. You could go round the whole planet, just jumping from Waterloo to Waterloo.

I found Waterloos with waterfalls, Waterloos in the jungle, Waterloos in snowy mountains and Waterloos with sandy white beaches. I couldn't figure out why anyone who wanted to live in a Waterloo would think—yes, Waterloo, but not the one with the big beach, or the one in the limitless white wastes of Siberia; no, the one with the flyover, handy for the New Strand Shopping Center.

DraxWorld gives you directions to anywhere, so it's not like it would be hard. If you were a proper grown-up and not just a stubbly boy—if you were my dad, for instance—all you'd have to do is fill your car with gas, turn left, turn right, go straight on and next thing you know: white beaches, snowy mountains, coral reefs. Truly, grown-upness is wasted on grown-ups.

* * *

When I got to school, Mrs. Sass (the headmistress) saw me in reception and said, "Ah . . . Tom?"

"Liam."

"Yes, of course. I'm Lorraine—come this way."

I remember thinking, Fancy her telling me her first name. Isn't that friendly? Mrs. Kendall never told us her first name when we were in Joan of Arc.

So "Lorraine" took me off to the staff room and started telling me the names of all the teachers. They all shook hands with me and said they were pleased to meet me. I was thinking, What a polite school! I wonder if they do this to every new kid. It must take ages. Then Lorraine said, "Everybody, this is Tom—sorry, Liam—Middleton, our new head of media studies." And she was pointing at me.

I know I should've put her right there and then, but someone gave me a mug of coffee and a custard cream and sat me down in a nice big easy chair. So I thought, I'll tell her later when I've eaten the biscuit.

Then Lorraine said, "We've got assembly this morning. I'll bring you up onto the stage and introduce you to the whole school. Do you have anything you'd like me to say about you—like what soccer team you support, or any special interests?"

I suppose that would have been a good time to say, "Very interestingly I'm not a teacher. I'm a Year Seven." But she just seemed so happy, so I said, "I like massively multiplayer online computer games."

She looked a bit blank.

"Like World of Warcraft. You know, where you have an avatar, and your avatar has skills and goes on quests?"

"Ah," said Lorraine, "skills. We are great believers in promoting skills here at Waterloo High."

"I've got a lot of skills," I said. "Of course, some of them aren't that useful in real life—like dragon taming. Some of them are illegal—like knife throwing. I think that's illegal."

"I think it probably is."

"I did try to persuade the headmistress in my last school to start a World of Warcraft club, but she just looked at me like I was an idiot."

Lorraine looked at me like I was an idiot.

Then the bell went. "We'd better go through to assembly. Maybe you should just introduce yourself. Don't worry about being interesting."

So that's how I ended up on the stage, standing just behind Mrs. Sass while she talked to the whole school. There were about eight people in the front row who knew me because they'd been at St. Joan of Arc Primary too, including Florida Kirby, who kept waving and making faces. Mrs. Sass said everyone was welcome and she hoped everyone had had a good summer and then something about a new registration procedure, and then she said, "And now I'd like to introduce you to a new member of staff. He's going to be teaching media studies and he'll be form tutor for Class Nine Mandela. This is Mr. Middleton. . . ."

And she pointed at me.

I stepped up to the microphone and said, "Thanks, Lorraine—sorry, Mrs. Sass." But everyone in the hall was already muttering, "Lorraine . . . her name's Lorraine . . ." and Lorraine was looking cross.

All these faces were looking up at me. Part of me was thinking, I really should think more about the consequences of my actions. Then this wouldn't happen to me. But another part of me was thinking, This is good.

I said, "Morning, everybody."

And everybody said, "Morning, sir."

Sir!

I said, "Has anyone here been to Waterloo near Liverpool?"

Twelve hundred hands shot up and waggled in the air like a salute. Looking out at them, I felt like the bad emperor in *Star Wars*. I took a breath and said, "Has anyone been to Waterloo in Belgium, scene of the original Battle of Waterloo in 1815?" No one. I said, "Siberia. Siberia is as big as Europe. It's got the largest freshwater lake in the world.

A lake so big it has its own species of dolphin. The ice is so thick that the railway runs over it. It's also got a town called Waterloo. Has anyone here been to Waterloo, Siberia?"

No one put their hand up.

"Why not?"

No one answered, but they all squirmed in their seats, as though going to Siberia was homework and they hadn't done it.

"Waterloo in Sierra Leone?"

No one had.

"Sierra Leone has lush rain forests and amazing history. Anyone?"

No one.

"Why!?"

They all squirmed again. "Why have we all been to the Waterloo with the bypass and the shopping mall when none of us has ever been to the Waterloo with the waterfall, the Waterloo in the jungle, the Waterloo by the frozen lake? Why? These places—they're not in Narnia. You don't have to find a magic wardrobe to get to them. They're not in Azeroth. You don't have to create an avatar and climb inside a computer. They're real places. You can go there by bus. Sometimes it'll take a lot of buses. But they're just there. They're part of your world."

Someone shouted, "Yes!"

I was amazed to see it wasn't one of the children; it was Mrs. Sass. I realize now that she thought I was being a bit metaphorical. She thought I was going to say something about how education opens up new worlds for you or something. But I didn't. I said, "Let's go!" No one moved. They all thought I was being metaphorical too. I said, "Come on. What are we doing here? Let's go. Come on. Follow me."

I don't know where that last bit came from. It just came out. It was part of the flow of the thing. I walked out down the middle of the hall toward the doors at the back. It took a minute, but somebody followed me. Then someone else. Then someone else and someone else and everyone followed me out of the hall, through the lower-school exit and into the playground.

The sun was shining. The birds were singing. I walked up to the gates and pushed. Nothing happened. Waterloo High is a high-security school. The gates are locked at nine a.m. and no one can get in or out without a swipe card. That's why there was a man in a leather jacket standing on the other side of the gates, talking into the intercom.

"I'm the new head of media studies," he was saying.

And over the intercom the secretary was saying, "I don't understand. You're already here. You're taking assembly."

By then Mrs. Sass was at the gate. She looked at the actual new head of media studies. Then she looked at me and she hissed, “Who are you?”

I did try to explain it all to her. I said, “I’m really sorry, Lorraine.”

“Don’t call me Lorraine anymore. It’s Mrs. Sass.”

“Yes, Mrs. Sass.”

“Why didn’t you tell me your real name?”

“I did.”

“But . . . well, you should have more sense, a big lad like you.”

When I got home Mom said, “So how did it go? First day at big school?”

I said, “All right.”

“Is that all you’ve got to say? All right?”

“No.”

“What else?”

“I’m starving.” Sometimes it’s better not to go into too much detail.

My Visible Friend

There were about ten million meetings and letters home about my "peculiar and disruptive" behavior at school assembly. Mrs. Sass decided that the problem was I had "poor social skills" because I was an only child. "He doesn't mix with the other children. He's an isolated figure on the playground."

Wouldn't you be an isolated figure if people followed you round, shouting, "Sir, sir!" or "Wolverine!" or yelling, "Hello up there!" a million times a day? I mean, what did they want me to do? Shrink?

Dad said, "You need to try and make some friends."

"I've got loads of friends. I've got twenty guild members just waiting to do my bidding."

"I'm talking about real life, not computers."

"I don't accept that distinction."

"That's exactly my point," said Dad. "You need a friend

who is visible to the naked eye."

The point about World of Warcraft is that the other players don't know how tall or short or fat or thin you are, they just accept you for what you are—namely, in my case, a highly skilled Night Elf with healing powers.

This wasn't enough for Mom and Dad. So they sent me to the Little Stars drama group. Every Saturday morning. Lisa—the girl who ran it—didn't seem impressed with my poor social skills. She sucked her teeth and looked me up and down and said, "We're really a children's theater group."

"He's twelve," said Dad.

"What? Mental age?"

"No. Physical age. And mental, I suppose. He's twelve—mentally, physically, emotionally, the lot. He's just a bit tall. And stubbly."

"Oh!" She looked like she didn't believe him. I showed her my passport.

"He's a clever lad," said Dad. "He's in Gifted and Talented."

"He's not exactly a *little* star though, is he?" said Lisa. "I suppose if we did *The Big Friendly Giant*, he'd be perfect. So"—she smiled—"why don't we do that then?"

So we did. Florida Kirby was already a fully paid-up Little Star. Lisa gave her the part of the giant's little friend, Sophie.

"The Sophie in the play," Florida said, "was named after

Sophie Dahl, the supermodel. So when I play Sophie, I'm playing a young supermodel." Florida always has to be a celebrity. When Lisa made us do a role play in which we had to act like we'd seen a ghost, Florida saw the ghost of Britney Spears. When we had to pretend to be a dog, she was Madonna's dog.

As we walked home through the Strand the first day Florida kept practicing her lines on me. The lines were mostly things like "You're huge!" "Goodness, you're tall!" or "You're proper gigantic!" and she said them all in her best Little Stars loud-and-clear voice. I sat down on one of the benches by the zen garden, just to be a bit less tall for a while.

"If we sit here," said Florida, "security will come and chase us. They hate kids hanging round this bench. They hate kids really."

But security didn't come and chase us. In fact, one of them walked past us and nodded at me.

"What's going on?" said Florida.

"They think," I explained, "that you are with me. And that I am your dad."

"No. You're kidding! Do they? Do they, honest?"

"Yes."

"But this is brilliant."

And she was right. We could do anything, so we did. That Saturday and every Saturday from then on we played on the lifts, messed about in the photo booth, went into Total Games and tried out all the new releases. We even went into Newz and Booze, which is "Strickly no unaccumpanid children under eny sercumstance's." Florida loved it in there because she could browse through all the celebrity magazines while I bought a newspaper to make myself look more dadly. Sometimes she used to give me a pound before we went inside so I could buy her chocolate.

I said, "Buy your own chocolate."

"Girls do not buy their own chocolate when they're out with their dads. Dads buy it for them."

She even tried to get me to buy her cigarettes.

"Dads don't buy their children cigarettes."

"My actual dad would. He'd do anything for me. He's going to buy me a pony."

"Ask your actual dad then."

Once I went in there without her and the woman behind the counter said, "Where's your little princess today then?"

How much did Florida love *that* when I told her. "Princess is brilliant. You have to call me Princess."

"I don't think so."

"Why not? My dad calls me Princess all the time."

"We'll talk about this another time," I said.

"Whoa, you really sounded like a dad when you said that."

"Thanks."

Another time she brought her little sister, Ibiza, with her. "Oh, another one," said the woman in Newz and Booze. "I didn't know you had two. I hope you don't mind me saying this, but it's lovely to see a young dad spending time with his girls the way you do. And they're both a credit to you. Aren't you lucky girls to have such a good dad?"

And she gave them a Chomp bar each.

It was a golden time and maybe we should have stopped there. But if you play a lot of games, then the moment you get good at something, that feels like Level One. You start itching to level up.

One day Lisa had to finish early because her dad was ill. We could have spent the time in the Strand doing all the usual things. Or we could have used the extra time to look for Level Two.

The 61 stops right outside the parish hall and goes all the way to Liverpool's celebrated city center. So there it was. The way to Level Two.

Being a grown-up in the Strand was fun. Being a grown-up in Liverpool's celebrated city center was totally cosmic. The moment we got off the bus a woman in a white miniskirt and a red sash came up, said hello, and gave me a free sample of a new yogurt drink. "Here," she said, "have a couple more for your little girl." We hadn't even finished drinking them when another woman gave me a free newspaper and another one—in a trouser suit—asked me if I had five minutes to answer some questions.

The questions were mostly about how we had got to town and what our favorite shops were. Then there were a few about what year I was born and what I did for a living. I gave her my dad's birthday and told her I was a taxi driver. She said, "Would you like to come in here with me and taste a new sandwich spread we're developing and on which we'd value your opinion?"

She took us to a really nice room and gave us free sandwiches and fizzy water. Afterward we had to fill in questionnaires and we were allowed to keep the pens. Florida asked for more sandwiches. The woman in the trouser suit laughed and said, "I guess that's all the feedback we need."

"So can we have some more then?"

"No."

Which is how we ended up near the world-famous waterfront, looking in the window of the Porsche showroom. Florida said, "That would be going too far, wouldn't it?"

"Let's find out." I was getting that Crispy New World feeling again.

It was my first time in a car showroom. I'd never seen a car on a carpet before. It was like being in the living room of the Posh Car Family. The cars looked smaller and glossier than they usually do. A man in a suit saw us come in and said, "Be with you in a minute, sir. Help yourself to coffee."

There was a coffee machine and a plate of biscuits—disappointingly mostly plain digestives. Florida nabbed the only Bourbon biscuit. Then she walked around dropping crumbs on their carpet. There was one really nice, sleek-looking car. Florida said, "Take a picture of me with your mobile."

"Why?"

"That's what dads do."

So she leaned on the hood and smiled while I took her picture. Straightaway the man in the suit was standing next to us. "I admire your taste," he said.

Florida said, "This is the Boxster. Wayne Rooney's got two like this, in red."

"He has indeed," said the man in the suit, "and he bought them both here. You're a very well-informed little girl." Then he asked me how old she was.

I said, "She's eleven." Then I thought I should say something grown-up so I said, "I'm not sure about this color."

"There's a red one like Wayne's over here. Come and have a look."

So I did.

"I've got to agree with you. A car like this was born to be red." It was nice of him to agree with me even though I didn't remember saying that. "She costs a bit . . ."

"I know." The price was written on the windshield.

". . . but she's worth it."

"Yeah. Oh. Yeah."

"Are you looking to buy or just looking?"

Yes, I know what I should've said. But "to buy" sounded older.

"Would you be bringing your old car in, in part exchange?"

"No. No, I like my old car. I'll probably keep my old car. It's a good car."

"I know the score. The other one's a family car. That's for when you're being a proper grown-up dad. This is for when you're playing racing cars. Isn't that right?" He winked at Florida. "Men, eh? We never grow up, do we?"

"He definitely hasn't," said Florida.

"Well," said the man in the suit, "let's pretend we have grown up. Just for a minute. What's your income?"

"I'm not sure. Varies really."

"You're right. You are so right. I'm too nosy. I mean you haven't even said you want her yet, have you?"

"No. No, I haven't."

"I'm always giving it the hard sell. A car like this, you should let it sell itself."

That's when Florida said, "Can we sit in it then?"

He looked at her for a second and she said, "Please?"

"Go on then."

We both got in. She whispered, "You should've told me to say please."

"You did say please."

"Yeah, but you should've told me before I got the chance. That's more dadlike."

"Okay."

The man in the suit looked in, winked at Florida and said, "Comfy?"

"Yeah," said Florida.

I said, "Yeah, what?"

"Yeah, thanks."

And then the man handed me the keys. "Go on," he said. "You know you're dying to. Just nudge her out onto the forecourt. See how she handles." Before I could say anything he was asking the other salesmen to move the other cars out of the way and open the big doors so I could take the car outside.

"I'll need to push the seat back a bit for you. You're a big lad, aren't you?"

I could've said, Yes, I am a big lad but that doesn't mean I'm old. I didn't say that. I said, "Thanks," and added, "mate."

"Have you got your license on you, Mr. . . . ?"

"Er . . . Digby. No. No, I haven't." I tried not to sound too happy about this.

"That's all right, Mr. Digby. I trust you. Thousands wouldn't."

He waved me into the seat, crouched down next to me and gave me a guided tour of the dashboard— "There's your MP3 player, your ergonomic seat thing, your satnav, in case you actually want to go somewhere."

I had a thought. "I've got DraxWorld on my phone. Can I hook that up to the satnav?"

He was impressed. He said, "Not sure. Give it a go."

I got DraxWorld up on my phone and chose a Waterloo.

"Waterloo," said the man. "No, this doesn't work. Waterloo's about fifteen minutes from here. This is showing a journey time of three days."

"Actually," I said, "that's Waterloo in Sierra Leone, Africa."

He looked at me like I was talking pure poetry. "Wow," he said, "Africa. And it's in your favorites? What would you do? Shoot down through France? Over the Pyrenees . . ." He was gone, imagining the whole journey in his head—the rivers, the mountains, the ferries, the desert. "Mr. Digby," he said, "you *deserve* this car. If I could, I'd give it you."

So I turned the key in the ignition. The car made a sound like a cat purring. The man stepped aside and pointed to the hood. “Engineering perfection.” He smiled.

It is at the moment, I thought. But in five minutes’ time it might well be a load of scrap metal. The thing about Level Two of course is that it has new and unexpected dangers. So you stand a much better chance of being killed.

I looked down at the pedals. I knew one of them was the accelerator. I just wasn’t quite sure which one. One lesson that World of Warcraft teaches you is that if you want to succeed on the next level, you need to acquire new skills. Don’t level up until you’ve skilled up. Sadly this was a lesson I had forgotten. I was pretty sure though that the accelerator was the one in the middle. I had my foot on it when the door on the passenger side opened and a very familiar voice said, “You. Out. Now. Come on.”

I probably didn’t mention this at the time, Dad, but, on balance, I was pleased to see you.

When I climbed out, you were shouting at the man in the suit, telling him that I could have been killed and asking him why they don’t check ages.

“How was I supposed to know?” wailed the man.

“By checking his license.” Good point, Dad.

“He didn’t have one.”

“Of course he hasn’t got one. He’s twelve years old.”

“Look, mate,” said the man in the suit, “don’t go blaming

me because your son's a freak."

I thought Dad was going to hit him then. He growled, "He is not a freak. He is normal. But tall."

"It wasn't just his height. It was the fact that he seemed to have a daughter."

Dad's got this little statue of St. Christopher stuck to his dashboard. When he was shoving me into the taxi on the way back from the town center I bumped against it and it rolled onto the floor.

"Pick that up," snapped Dad.

"Okay, okay. You've knocked the baby Jesus off his back."

"Just don't talk to me, Liam."

I said okay, but there was something I wanted to ask him. I waited till we were on the Dock Road, then I said, "How did you know where we were?"

"I'm your dad," he said. "If you act funny, I notice. If you get on an unexpected bus instead of going home, I follow you, even if that means turning down fares and having the boss bawling at me on the radio. I'm your dad. It's what dads do."

Thinking about that now makes me wonder if you're out there, somewhere behind us, charging after us through the wastes of space in your taxi. But no. No taxi would be able to generate the necessary escape velocity.

* * *

In case you are interested, by the way, this is how Dad located us that day. When he gave me his old phone, he bought himself a new one but he kept his old number. So there were two phones—phone one (Dad's) and phone two (mine)—with the same identity. So, if he was ever worried about me, he could fire up DraxWorld and request "present position of phone two," and that would tell him where I was.

So my phone looked like a phone but it was really an electronic tag.

Because we shared a phone number, I used to get all Dad's messages from Pine Planet, telling me that my new kitchen units were ready for collection, and Dad used to get messages from members of my World of Warcraft guild saying stuff like, "Beenattackedbydragons—needyrhealingpowersnow!" and "Captured fifty goblins. Kill? or hold for ransom?" A nervous person might've thought, Blimey, we're being invaded by mythical creatures, and maybe gone and hidden away in the woods behind the golf course. Dad just thought, This phone's gone funny. I'll turn it off and turn it on again.

That's Dad's solution to any technological problem. Microwave, satnav, computer, dishwasher—turn it off and back on again and it'll be okay. To be fair, it usually works. I'd try it now, but I'm not sure this rocket has an Off switch.

My Planet Panda Pop

The school-assembly incident was bad. The Porsche-showroom incident was like being killed and sent back to Level One with no spare lives. "All we wanted," said Mom, "was for you to learn some social skills."

"Social skills?" said Dad. "Well, let's see—he got a little girl to pose as his daughter, and he persuaded a salesman to lend him a Porsche. He's got social skills. He's got *too many* social skills. We asked him to learn some and he learned too many. That's the problem."

It turned out that Dad was right about visible friends being different from cyberfriends. If someone doesn't turn up on Warcraft, you can always just recruit someone else. But when I walked through the New Strand Shopping Center on Saturday mornings, even though there were thousands of people there, it was really noticeable that none of them was Florida.

* * *

Mom got really stressed about the whole thing. "Liam," she kept saying, "what are we going to do with you?"

Dad looked on the Internet for self-help groups for people with unusual problems. About an hour later he came back and said, "What about this—popular coastal resort, Tunisia? A hundred and fifty pounds a head."

"Tunisia's a bit far," said Mom. "I was hoping there'd be a group in the library."

"No, I'm talking about a holiday. That's what we need, isn't it? The three of us. Go somewhere no one knows us. And just unwind."

I was completely excited about this. I'd never been abroad before. I spent the whole week reading holiday brochures and even went with Mom and Dad to the travel agent, which was a disaster because when I get completely excited I talk too much. For instance, when Tunisia was mentioned, I said, "Yes. Four-star accommodation, all meals *and* we could go and see the Sahara Desert!"

Mom said, "The Sahara Desert? You are joking. The Sahara Desert is a desert. People get lost in deserts. They starve to death and see mirages and get eaten alive by ants. Oh no, no, no, no. We're not going to a desert."

The travel-agent woman said, "If you did choose the *optional* desert excursion, Mrs. Digby, you would be accompanied by our trained local staff in a fully air-conditioned coach. It's a very well-organized trip."

"No one ever," said Mom, "INTENDS to get eaten alive by ants. But Accidents Happen. Especially in the Sahara Desert. What else have you got?"

"Tenerife is already quite warm."

Although it is politically part of Spain, the island of Tenerife is off the coast of Africa and is therefore hot all the year round. Especially in the south. It's more rainy in the north because of this big pointy mountain in the middle of the island. It's so tall that it has snow on top, even in the summer. It's called Teide. Mom looked interested when I told her all of this. I probably should've stopped just there and not gone on to mention that Teide isn't just an ordinary mountain.

"A volcano!?" said Mom.

"An *extinct* volcano," said the woman from the travel agency, very quickly.

"Extinct or dormant?" said Mom, surprising everyone with her unexpected geological knowledge.

"What's the difference?" asked the travel-agent lady.

"The difference," said Mom, "between life and death."

The travel-agent woman held up a brochure for Florida. "Very popular." She smiled, without going into detail.

Mom looked at me. I said nothing.

She looked at the travel agent, who just kept smiling.

She looked at Dad. He tried to keep smiling too. But she raised an eyebrow and he just can't cope with that. In the end he admitted, "Alligators."

After that there was Turkey (earthquakes), Cyprus (poisonous triggerfish), Italy (the Mafia) and Greece (shipwrecks). Then we were standing outside the shop with Mom taking a deep breath and saying, "Well, I haven't even gone anywhere and I'm already glad to be home."

They decided to forget about the holiday and redecorate the kitchen instead. Dad pointed out that a holiday only lasted a week or two whereas a new kitchen would last forever. So instead of going on a well-organized, air-conditioned trip of the Sahara, we went to Nothing But Drainers and looked at granite work surfaces.

"This one's a bit pricey," said the man, "but you get what you pay for and this is real Italian granite."

It was mostly blue. I remember looking at it, thinking, That's igneous rock. That came from way underground in Italy. That drainer has had a more exciting life than I have.

Dad said, "What d'you think, Liam?"

"Good. You can't go wrong with igneous. It is igneous, isn't it?"

The man said, "I don't think so. These are new in today

from our supplier in Turin."

I said, "It's made of crystallized magma."

"No, son. This is real Italian granite. It's not made at all."

"It was made by magma bubbling up from the Earth's mantle millions of years ago. The molten magma cooled in the crust and turned into crystals, then probably sat, being squeezed into flat beds for about a billion years until it was dug up by Italians. All that trouble and then it's chopped up and sent to Nothing But Drainers, where my mom will look at it for five minutes and say, 'I'm not sure about this color.'"

The man looked at Dad. Dad just shrugged. "He's in Gifted and Talented. At school. They study this kind of thing. Last month it was global warming."

Mom said, "He is right though. I'm not sure about this color."

Not only was I not allowed to go to Tunisia, I wasn't even allowed to walk home by myself anymore. Mom and Dad took to meeting me at school and escorting me home, like a prisoner. They would have banned me from Little Stars too except everyone else had done so much work on *The BFG* that it wouldn't be fair if it had to be canceled.

Lisa tried to be nice about it. "You're the star," she said, "so you get your own dressing room." Then she shoved me into this cupboardy thing just behind the stage. There was one chair, no window, a packet of pickled-onion flavor Space Ranger crisps and a blue Panda Pop. Space Rangers are the cheapest crisps that money can buy. They are crisps, but only until you put them in your mouth. The moment they make contact with your tongue they stop being crisps and become soggies. The flavor is sort of optional in that it seems to fall off the crisps and make a powdery sludge at the bottom of the bag, which you can scroop up with your finger if you like. Blue Panda Pops are supposedly raspberry flavored, but the flavor is irrelevant as they are so fizzy that when you drink them all your senses close down and your brain just shouts, "FIZZY!" Later on you belch a lot, which is fine if you're playing the BFG, as he's quite a belchy character.

I remember sitting in that cupboard, feeling like the rest of the world had completely vanished and that I was now orbiting the sun entirely on my own, on a chair. Planet Panda Pop. Sitting in a tiny enclosed space eating strange chemicals. It turns out that Little Stars was outstanding training for astronauts.

During the interval, I just messed about on DraxWorld. At first I checked "location of phone one"—so I could see where Dad was. He was in the audience. Then I looked at all the Waterloos in the world, trying to decide on a favorite. I was just tossing up between Waterloo in Sierra Leone and Waterloo in Trinidad and Tobago when the phone rang. It was a woman with a very friendly voice saying, "Hi, I'm calling on behalf of Drax Communications. We've noticed you have a very interesting pattern of use and we'd like to ask you a few questions if you have some minutes."

I had about two and a half minutes to the beginning of Act Two.

"Can I just ask you, have you actually been to any of the following places which appear in your recent searches—Waterloo, Sierra Leone?"

"No."

"Waterloo, Siberia?"

"No."

"Waterloo, Belgium?"

"No."

"Do you have any plans to visit these places in the near future?"

"Yeah," I said, "all of them. I don't know how near the future is though."

"We also noticed that your recent searches include many theme parks and rides."

"Oh. Yes. Alton Towers. EuroDisney. Six Flags. Mountain—"

"Pretty well all the theme parks in the world, in fact.

What is it you like about theme parks?"

"The Crispy New World feeling you get after you've been on a thrill ride. I love that."

"So you go on the rides with your children?"

She thought I was a grown-up and she couldn't even see me! I deepened my voice a bit and said, "That's right. Yeah."

"How old is your child?"

"Eleven."

"Lovely. Thank you. And one last thing—as a dad, how would you summarize your philosophy of child rearing?"

"My what?"

"What do you want most for your children?"

"Well . . ." I don't remember thinking about it. I just came out with this: "I want my children to think of the whole world as their thrill ride."

"Oh," said the woman. "What a beautiful thought."

And I was thinking, Yes, it is a lovely thought. I wonder where it came from.

"Thank you, Mr. Digby, for talking to me. We'll be in touch very soon."

She hung up. In World of Warcraft, when you defeat an enemy you can take their stuff: their money, their armor, things like that. But sometimes it turns out they've got something you weren't expecting—like a magic ability or a bottle of the Elixir of the Mages. And you can feel the extra power surge through you. That's how I felt at the end of that call. I knew something cosmic was going to happen.

A few minutes later, Lisa knocked on the door, shouting, "BFG onstage, please!"

As we were walking up to the wings, I got a text. Lisa snarled, "Turn off your mobile, for goodness' sake."

"In a second."

"In fact, give it to me."

"Okay, yeah, whatever," I said with a giant smile. I was smiling because of the text:

You have been selected to take part in a very special competition, with a prize that will make you into a hero in the eyes of your children. Infinity Park is a unique new theme park in China, packed with astonishing, innovative attractions, including the Biggest Thrill Ride in the History of the World—the Rocket. We are offering four fathers and their children the chance to travel to the park, experience the rides and visit local landmarks.

Don't miss your chance to become the Greatest Dad Ever. Call this secret number tomorrow before midday GMT to find out if you are one of the four lucky winners. Please do not disclose this number to anyone else.

All you have to do is get put through.

* * *

I was still smiling after the play was over and everyone had finished clapping. Lisa said I was the friendliest-looking Big Friendly Giant she'd ever seen. Mom said, "I loved it. You looked so *happy* up there!"

I waited till we were getting into the car and then I showed Dad the text. "China . . . the Biggest Thrill Ride in the History of the World . . . your chance to become the Greatest Dad Ever." I got that Crispy New World feeling just reading it.

I expected Dad to jump up and down with excitement and say, "Get the suncream, Liam." Inexplicably he didn't. He shook his head and said, "No one really wins those things."

"Well, someone must win them. Otherwise they wouldn't be allowed to advertise them. Of course someone wins them. Come on, it's just a phone call."

"Yes, a long, long phone call. This is just a trick to get you to spend loads of money calling a premium-rate phone number. And when you do, there's nothing at the other end except a voice saying 'Please hold' and playing some nice classical music. And they collect the money for the call."

"But you've been specially selected."

"Yeah. Me and ten million others."

He deleted the message.

* * *

We walked home past the shopping center. I looked up but you couldn't see any stars. I remember thinking, I'll probably never get out of Bootle as long as I live. It's funny to think I am now at this moment farther away from Bootle than any other living human.

That night Dad wanted us all to play Monopoly in the new kitchen. Monopoly! Has *anyone ever* played Monopoly to the end? Don't most people just sort of slip into a kind of boredom coma after a few goes and wake up six months later with a handful of warm hotels? If it had been Risk or Cluedo, that would have been something, but Monopoly!

"Sit down," he said. "It'll be nice. All of us together. We haven't played a game for ages."

I said, "Monopoly is not a game."

"Well, here's the dice and here's the board—how is that not a game?"

"It's not a game because NOTHING IS HAPPENING. In Monopoly you can ask someone else to take your go for you while you go to the toilet and it won't make any difference. Can you imagine asking someone else to take your go in chess, or Risk, or soccer? I'll tell you what Monopoly is. Monopoly is my life—going round and round the same streets over and over again with not enough money."

"So," said Dad, "you don't want to play then?"

"No, I don't." I got up. I was going to go and play a few hours of Warcraft.

"It's always an anticlimax," said Mom, "when you're in a play or something and then it ends."

"You don't want to play a little game of Monopoly with your real live mom and dad?" said Dad. "But you'll play all night with your invisible Warcraft friends."

"I haven't got any real live friends left, have I?"

"Maybe you would have if you weren't always coaxing them into illegal situations involving high-powered sports cars."

"Oh now," said Mom, "he isn't *always* doing that. He only did it once."

"And isn't once enough?!"

They were still discussing this when I logged into Azeroth and summoned my guild—the Wanderlust Warriors.

We were crossing the Blasted Lands with a caravan of traders when the door opened and Dad looked in. "Listen," he said, "I'm sorry about earlier. If you don't want to play Monopoly, that's fine. I'll play Warcraft."

"Oh. Thanks. But it doesn't really work like that."

"How does it work then?"

So I tried to explain Warcraft to Dad, but honestly—where

do you begin? He didn't even know what an avatar was.

I said, "Like when we play Monopoly and you are always the top hat? Well, it's like that, only more complicated. That's me on the screen, look, that elf."

He squinted at the screen. There were hundreds of avatars across the vast desert of the Blasted Lands. I showed him which one was mine and I introduced him to all my other guild members. We're mostly very heavily armed Night Elves. I think he was impressed.

"You see," I said, "in Monopoly, you get as much money as you can, right? And that's it. In here you have to get money. And health. And experience. And skills. And then . . . you use them. For a quest."

"What kind of quest?"

"Well, there's all kinds. Some of them are dangerous and complicated and some are simple. And you meet hazards and monsters. Sometimes serious monsters—so you run away or get help. And sometimes trivial monsters—so you fight them. And if you complete the quest, you gain experience and new skills and maybe some strength and wealth. So then you can level up . . ."

"What?"

"See, I'm a Level Forty elf, but what I want to be is a Level Seventy elf. Then I can Engage with really serious monsters. When you Engage, that's called an Instance. We're having a bit of an instance right now with this dragon."

The dragon had ambushed us, but the Wanderlust Warriors stood their ground and fought like a well-oiled machine. Soon the dragon was dead. So were two of my Warriors, but that was okay because I've got healing powers. I brought them back to life and we looted the dragon's hoard.

That's what was happening in my head. Of course, to Dad it just looked like I was sitting there clicking the mouse so fast it sounded like castanets.

"Cosmic!" I yelled. "Look what we found: Elixir of the Mages. If you use that just before an instance, it doubles your brain power."

"This," said Dad, "is not a game. This is a career."

"But it's good on here because people just accept you for what you are."

"Namely an elf with magical healing powers. Is that what you really are, Liam?"

"No, but in-game, if I have experience and strength and stuff, I can go out on quests and do things. In-life, you can look like a grown-up and shave like a grown-up and be Gifted and Talented and everything, and you've still got to sit in a class full of kids who call you 'freak' and 'Wolverine' and stuff."

Dad nodded his head like it all made sense to him. Then

he got my profile up so he could have a proper look at my avatar.

"It says here he's shorter than average."

"If you're short you get extra agility. Plus you can sneak up on people."

Dad said, "A shorter-than-average magical being with lots of friends. Well . . . that's a very nice avatar. Good night."

I did offer to tell him something about the history of Azeroth and who the Horde were and about the Alliance, but he said, "That's enough for one night, thanks all the same. You get back to your quest. Don't stay up too late—you've got school."

It was only when he'd gone that I noticed he'd left his phone on my desk. And only when I picked it up that I remembered that my phone was a clone of his. So the number he'd deleted from my in-box should still be there in his. It was. I copied it back into my phone.

I Am on Hold

I made the call on the bus to school next day. I remember looking out of the window at all the people: queuing outside the post office, standing at the pedestrian crossing, going in and out of 24-hour Tesco. None of them looked to me like they'd been specially selected. I was going to win. I dialed.

The woman with the friendly voice answered right away. "Drax Communications. D'you want the opportunity to be the Greatest Dad Ever?"

"Yeah, I do. I really do. I was thinking about it all night. . . ." I talked for about a minute before I realized she was a recording.

". . . if you accept the terms and conditions of this competition, please press the star key now."

I did.

"We'll take your call as soon as we can. In the meantime,

please hold. Remember: all you have to do is get put through."

They started playing classical music. They were still playing when the bus pulled up at the school gates half an hour later. Every now and then the music would stop and the friendly-voiced woman would say, "Your call means a lot to us. Please hold." There must be a lot of people in the queue. Maybe Dad was right. Maybe I wasn't that special.

I was walking in through the school gates when I got a text alert: "Yes! We have our 1st winner!"

Yes!? What's "Yes!" about that exactly?

Our first winner is Klaus from Hamburg in Germany, and his daughter Anna. Anna's two great passions are thrill rides and helping others, says her father. "She once spent twelve hours on the Space Mountain roller coaster at EuroDisney in order to raise money for a local hospital. She hopes to get people to sponsor her to ride the Rocket and so raise money for children who were injured in wars around the world. When her school friends heard about this, they wanted to help her. We knew there might be a problem getting through to the number so they all came to school early and all called the number simultaneously. A boy got through and gave the phone to Anna immediately. She is a worthy winner."

In other words, she cheated.

* * *

I was still on hold during registration. Registration's a noisy business so no one noticed the music. But first lesson was math with Ms. Jewell, and math with Ms. Jewell is always full of long silences, for instance:

Ms. Jewell:	**Square root of sixty-four?**
Class:	**Long silence.**
Ms. Jewell:	**Anybody? Anybody at all.**
Class:	**More long silence.**

So this morning I tried to answer all her questions, just to keep up the noise level and stop her noticing the phone. When she asked something about calculating the volume of a cylinder. I shouted, "Miss, miss . . ."

"Liam, there is no need to shout, 'Miss, miss,' if no one else is offering to answer the question. There is no need to try to attract my attention if you have no competition."

"Yes, miss. Anyway, miss, it's pi times the—"

"Thank you, Liam. I already know the answer. I already know *you* know the answer. I'm hoping to find out if anyone else knows the answer."

"Wayne probably knows, miss. He's good at math, miss, but he doesn't always have the confidence to put his—"

"Liam, I'm only too happy to hear your thoughts on geometry. I don't want your thoughts on your fellow pupils."

"Just going back to the volume of the cylinder then, miss, isn't it—"

"Don't go back to it, Liam. Let someone else have a go."

"Yes, miss."

"So . . . volume of a cylinder. Anyone? Anyone at all?"

Long pause. But not silence. A tinny little orchestra fiddling away.

She frowned. She prowled up and down. You could see that she thought it might be in the next room. Or in her head. Finally she said, "Can anyone else hear music? Or are the angels finally coming to carry me away?"

I laughed at this—probably too loud and definitely too long. No one else joined in but everyone did stare at me—including Ms. Jewell, who stared at me and then at my pocket. "It's Holst, isn't it?" she said.

I said, "No, miss, it's me," thinking, Who's Holst?

"This music was written by Gustav Holst. It's called *The Planets*. It's not the usual rubbish. Why're you playing it?"

"Well, miss, I saw a thing on TV about how if you play classical music in the background your brain really likes it and it makes extra pathways through your synapses. You can get brainier just by listening to classical music. It definitely works, miss—look how many questions I've answered this morning. . . ."

She was sort of humming along to the music now. I took

the phone out so she could hear better and asked, "Why's it called *The Planets*, miss?" I know this was cynical. But she's a teacher. She loves questions.

Ms. Jewell talked nonstop for the whole lesson about music, about Greek mythology and about the solar system. At one point she tried to explain just how far away Neptune was, and everyone gasped. And then she said, "And it's a near neighbor compared to the stars. . . ," and she did a massive calculation on the board to show how far away the nearest star was in both kilometers and light-years. It was the best lesson she ever gave us.

But I was still on hold at the end of it.

I did get another text alert though:

Our second winner is Samson Two Toure from Waterloo in Sierra Leone. Samson Two is the cleverest boy in the country. Recently his class was given a geography project about irrigation. Some of the other boys got A grades. Samson Two's project was so good that the government bought it. His father says, "It is important to push your children hard to fulfill their ambitions. Samson Two and I have fun setting achievement targets. For instance, on his tenth birthday he set himself the target of becoming president of our country. I set him the target of winning this competition to ride the Rocket and he did it by writing a computer program that bypassed the 'on hold' part of the phone call and put him straight through to the operator. Although he is not interested in fairground rides, he is looking forward to this opportunity to study one of the Wonders of the World."

I'm sorry, but if you already live in the Waterloo in Sierra Leone, instead of the Waterloo near Bootle, then you really don't need to go and see the Wonders of the World. Because you already are one of the Wonders of the World—you've got jungles and rivers instead of gaso-meters and bypasses. It's like the Grand Canyon wanting to come and look at the crack in my bedroom ceiling.

Still two lucky winners left to go. During the kerfuffle between lessons the next one was announced:

Our third winner is Max Martinet of Lille in France. Max's father believes in discipline. "So many children today are allowed to run wild," he says. "Not Max. I insist that he does exactly what he is told to do. If children are bad, you must punish them. If they are good, you must reward them. Max does as he is told. I told him to win this competition and he did."

See? All these other kids are getting help from their parents. What's my dad doing? Valeting the taxi.

* * *

The next lesson was media studies with Mr. Middleton, who blatantly hates me. We watched a DVD about the history of washing-powder adverts. No one noticed my phone playing in the background. I wondered how my credit was holding up. I'd now been on hold for three hours. Did it make me want to give up? No. What made me want to give up was the next text message. There were only going to be four winners in the competition, and this was the fourth:

We have a new winner: Hasan Xanadu from Bosnia. Hasan's father, Edhem, says, "Childhood is a happy time, and how can we be happy if we don't have the things we want? So I give Hasan everything he wants. After all, it's only money. And I can always get more money. For instance, he really loves thrill rides and he wanted to be the first ever to ride the Rocket. So I found the number of the girl who won it for charity. I phoned her and I offered to give the charity twice as much money as she could raise with sponsors. Simple! Everyone has their price!"

If the competition was over, then the music should stop and the lines should be closed. But the music was still playing. Then I realized that if he'd bought the German girl's place, then he wasn't the fourth winner.

He was a replacement first winner.

There was still one chance left.

And now the music had stopped and there was a ringing sound. I was being put through! I pulled the phone out of my pocket and got ready to speak.

A hand snatched the phone out of my hand. It was Mr. Middleton.

I pleaded with him not to hang up. "I'm in a queue, sir. I have been since eight o'clock this morning."

"No mobiles in class—an invariable rule and basic good manners. You should know that."

"Please don't hang up."

I could hear a friendly woman's voice talking on the phone. I was through!

He snapped the phone shut and smiled. "Tell me," he said, "what was important about the new ideas that Omo used to promote their washing powder in the 1960s?"

"What was important about them?"

"I'll give you a clue. Suds. Longer-lasting suds. Now then. Anything? No. You weren't listening to me, were you? What were you listening to? Little voices in your head? Or on your mobile? Maybe you'd like to tell the rest of us what they were saying."

It was a Level Seventy Monster Question, the kind you're supposed to walk away from. But I Engaged instead. I said, "Recent studies have shown that the chances of an asteroid hitting Earth any time in the next hundred years are five thousand to one. Blatantly the odds get stronger with every day that passes. A big enough asteroid could cause total global extinction. And therefore, it doesn't matter how long your suds last. And it doesn't matter if you've been specially selected or not."

Sometimes you don't need to take the Elixir of the Mages first. Sometimes if you simply step up to the monster, the elixir just comes.

He sent me out of the class.

Fathers Have Children

That was the night I finally took down my "It's Your Solar System" glow-in-the-dark mobile. It wasn't even astronomically accurate. It still had Pluto on it. Everyone knows that Pluto's not a planet anymore. It's something a bit too big for an asteroid, but too small for a planet. It's nothing.

Like someone who's too big to be a kid and too young to be an adult.

Then the phone rang.

A friendly voice said, "Hi. Drax Communications. Still want to be the World's Best Dad?" This time I waited for the options to come up. But they didn't. There was a pause and the friendly voice said, "Hello? Mr. Digby?"

"Oh. What? Yeah. Yeah, that's me. Who's that?"

"Dr. Dinah Drax here. I've been waiting for your call."

"*You*'ve been waiting for *my* call?!"

"Yes."

"But I tried to call this morning and I was on hold for about a year. I thought there must've been a million people in the queue."

"But I told you that you were specially selected. Didn't you believe me?"

"Yeah. But . . . the on-hold thing went on so long."

"I really wanted to share that piece of music with you."

"Well . . . thanks. I enjoyed it."

"And to find out how patient you were. Patience will be an essential quality on this trip."

"Oh, I can be patient. Really. I can sit for hours."

"Good. Well, Mr. Digby, you're through."

"That is completely cosmic."

"A car will collect you from your registered address at oh-eight hundred on Tuesday morning—"

"Dr. Drax . . . the Rocket . . . What kind of ride is it? Is it a reverse bungee? Or a roller coaster? Or—"

"Wait and see. That's one of the ways in which you can exercise your patience. Now tell me a little bit about the child you'll be bringing. . . ."

I'd completely forgotten that dads have children.

" . . . I do hope it's a girl. We're very short on girls."

"Oh. She's a girl then. Definitely. Anything you say."

"And what's her name?"

"Who?"

"Your daughter, Mr. Digby."

"My daughter?" Time to Engage. I said the name of the only daughter I'd ever had. I said, "It's Florida. Her name is Florida."

If Liverpool city center was Level Two, a secret location in China must be Level Fifty at least. I wasn't going to make the same mistake as last time. This time I was going to skill up before leveling up. In World of Warcraft you can have weapon skills, gathering skills or trade skills. You can have mining skills too, but they're a bit rubbish and you have to buy a pickax.

If I was going on a quest disguised as Florida's dad, I would need dad skills.

I went through all the books on my dad's bedside table. They were mostly color charts of quick-drying low-odor bathroom paints with mad names like Antarctic Glow, but there was one called *Talk to Your Teen*, which was all about how to trick your teenage son or daughter into talking to you.

Un.

Be.

Liev.

Able.

It was like finding the cheat sheet for Orbiter IV. Except it wasn't Orbiter IV; it was My Life. Look at this:

> *Does your teen sometimes seem sulky and uncommunicative? Meals are the most natural place for conversation to flow. To create the best possible conditions for this, you should turn off the television before eating and try to serve fiddly food. Fiddly food keeps everyone at the table longer. Whereas a pizza can be dispensed with in a matter of minutes, a plate of spaghetti can keep a hungry teen at the table for fully half an hour.*

In other words, meals are traps. Except what sane person would bait a trap with pasta?

It also said:

> *It's very important to show an interest in their world. Ask them about their friends, their music, their books and their computer games.*

So he was never interested in the history of Azeroth or the Wanderlust Warriors' weapons at all! He was just keeping me talking.

I should've realized this before, because when I carefully monitored my dad's conversations for several days, I discovered that they can all be broken down into five headings, namely:

1. How we got there.
2. What the parking was like.
3. What it was like in the old days.
4. Something thoughtful which it made you think.
5. Something to do with last night's soccer.

For instance, on the Saturday morning we went to the New Strand to look for new handles to put on the new kitchen cupboards. We didn't find any (though we did get an amusing cactus holder, shaped like a donkey). This is what Dad said:

1. The main road was so choked, we'd've been better off walking.
2. Two pounds to park for two hours! And it takes you half an hour to find a space.
3. In the old days, if the shop didn't have the right door handles for your cupboards you came home empty-handed. Nowadays, with shopping malls and what have you, if they haven't got door handles, you buy a cactus holder. It makes you think . . .
4. . . . are we really any happier now than we were then? Are we happier because we've got a cactus holder? It's not like we've got a cactus.

5. It's no good scoring lots of goals if you also concede lots of goals. We need a terrifying central defender.

These five headings apply to anything. For instance, if my dad ever did go to Azeroth, he'd probably say:

1. We took the Deeprun Tram to Stormwind (Dwarven District).
2. The tram is free. It's very reliable and you don't have to worry about parking. On the other hand, it was raided by the undead Scourge and a lot of us were killed. Luckily my guild companions have healing powers.
3. There was no such place as Azeroth when we were little. If we wanted to play a fantasy game we had to use sticks for swords and run round on pretend horses. The sticks really hurt.
4. We looked stupid, but we did get lots of fresh air.
5. Money has spoiled soccer. Players now spend more time advertising hair products than they do training.

I felt I'd mastered Level One of Being a Dad. Now I had to get myself a daughter.

You'll Like It When You Get There

The first person I thought of to be my daughter was obviously Florida. After all, she already had extensive pretending-to-be-Liam's-daughter experience and had gained lots of pretending-to-be-Liam's-daughter skills.

On the other hand, her main pretending-to-be-Liam's-daughter experience was me nearly putting her in incredible danger during that whole Porsche incident. So I knew I'd probably need to coax her slightly.

When I tried talking to her in school she either totally blanked me (but then she always did blank me in school) or hissed at me like an angry cobra. When I tried phoning her—calls from my number were barred. When I tried emailing and MSNing her, messages bounced back. I tried sitting by the Strand water fountain. She never came by. I think I saw her once, but she saw me first and ducked inside the Leaning Tower of Pizza.

That's okay. If you need new equipment for a quest, you have to work for it. You have to dig for gold or grind away, fighting trolls and looting their possessions. You have to keep going until you've got what you need.

The one place where Florida had to talk to me was Little Stars. That Saturday Lisa made us get into pairs—a boy and a girl—and asked us to be father and daughter. Florida tried to avoid me but I came up behind her and said, "You could be Bryce Dallas Howard, star of *Spider-Man 3*. And I'll be your father, Ron Howard, director of *Apollo 13* and *The Da Vinci Code*."

"Which one was she in *Spider-Man 3*?"

"She's the girl in Dr. Connor's quantum-mechanics class who falls in love with him and later on he saves her from a falling crane. That's in the film. Originally, she went to the same school as him and she was his first love and she dies when Green Goblin throws her off the bridge. But that was just in the comics."

"I remember. She was blond. And her dad is famous too?"

She didn't know many celebrity father-daughter combinations and she didn't want to let this one go.

Lisa was saying, "And Daddy's got his daughter a treat. It's up to you what the treat is. But the daughter really likes it. I want to see happy acting, and surprised acting, and also two people who really know each other type of acting. And for the boys, some older-person acting—but don't overdo it. No old-man acting. You don't have to be *old* old to be a dad."

As soon as we started working on it Florida said, "Okay. So you're my famous film-director dad and the surprise is a part in your new film."

"I'm the dad. It's up to me what the surprise is."

Straightaway she was suspicious. "What is it then?"

"You'll see."

When it was our turn, it went like this:

Florida: **Hi, Dad, how were things at the film set today?**

Me: **Pretty neat, I guess, Bryce. I have a present for you.**

Florida: **Oh Dad, you shouldn't have. Wait, I know what it is—a part in your new film.**

Me: **No.**

Florida: **But you said—**

Me: **Well, it's not that. It's nicer than that.**

Florida: **Remember I earned loads of money by being in Spider-Man 3, so I have got practically everything a girl could want.**

Me: It's a little holiday—to a theme park—just the two of us.

Florida looks puzzled.

Me: It's a brand-new theme park. One of the rides is going to be the Best Ride in the World and we've got an invitation. [Adding in a whisper] This is real. Honest. I won a competition.

An extremely long pause. After a while Lisa said, "Is that it?"

Florida [stops looking puzzled and looks annoyed]: Dad, I can't go.

Me: Yes, you can. It'll be great. It's a once-in-a-lifetime thing. Pack your bags and come with me. Don't miss out.

Florida: I've got so much acting to do. So many commitments. I can't go. You must know that.

Me: But this is a once-in-a-lifetime experience. It's the very first day the theme park is open. You're going to be the first person on the rides! REALLY.

Florida: No.

Me: You'll like it when you get there.

Florida:	**No, I won't.**
Me:	**Yes, you will. Just you and me together, father and daughter, like old times.**
Florida:	**Together?**
Me:	**Yeah. Me and you, father and daughter. What d'you think? We never spend any time together now because you're always acting and I'm always directing films.**
Florida:	**Well, you should have said so earlier. I can't go now.**
Me:	**Why not?**

Another long pause. Lisa said, "Go on, Florida, tell us why not."

Florida:	**Because I don't want to. I already said that. Can't you get it into your thick head?**
Me:	**I was only trying to give you something nice. I thought you'd like to go on a holiday with your dad.**
Florida:	**Well, I wouldn't. Because I'm too busy doing other things.**

Lisa said the drama was very real and also very moving. "I felt very sorry for the dad, who obviously wanted to spend more time with his daughter but she was too busy to make time for him. And Liam, you were so . . . dad-like. You really were like a real dad. Like my own dad, in fact. He was always saying I'd like it when I got there and . . . I'm sorry." She had to stop talking because she was crying. In the end she did this huge sniff, looked at Florida and said, "And, Florida, you were very good too. You were . . . oh!" And then she ran out of the room.

While she was out, I tried quickly to tempt Florida with the trip. "First in. First go of all the rides. Exclusive entry. No queues. Free food."

"Why? Why did they invite you?"

"It was a prize. I was specially selected."

"And why would you want me to come?"

"Well, the prize was for a father and child."

"So?" For a second she didn't seem to get it. Then it hit her. "Oh! Oh. No, no, no, no, no . . ."

"Why not? We used to do it all the time."

"Exactly. We used to do it all the time; then we nearly had a car crash."

"We did not nearly have a car crash. We sat in a car and then my dad turned up."

"And what if your dad hadn't turned up? No, no, no, no, no. No."

* * *

She was still saying no when the lesson was over and we were hurrying through the Strand. I said, "Hey, d'you want to go to Newz and Booze and look at the magazines like we used to?"

"No. I've got to pick my little brother up from the childminder's."

"I didn't know you had a little brother."

"You don't know a lot of things."

Florida's brother is three, he's got loads of curly hair and when we picked him up from the childminder's he was wearing an anorak with the hood pulled up really tight around his head and carrying a stick.

"He's a knight at the moment," said Florida. "The hood is his helmet. The stick is his sword. If I tell him you're a dragon, he will kill you." The little boy held my hand.

"What's your name?" I said to him.

"Orlando."

"My mom and dad went there on their honeymoon. Orlando in America. That's where Disney World is. And Sea World. And the Magic Kingdom."

"This place I won tickets for—it's better than all those places."

"How do you know?"

"Because it's got this ride called the Rocket. It's the

greatest ride in the history of the world."

"Why don't you get your own dad to go?"

"He doesn't want to. Anyway, *I'm* the dad—that's the whole point."

"Liam, look, you look a bit old for your age, but no one's really going to think you're my dad. I'm only three months younger than you! And you don't *act* like a dad. Dads don't steal fast cars."

"I didn't steal it. I sat in it. Anyway, I've been studying."

"Liam, what are you on about?"

"I've been getting dad skills. I've made a scientific study of my dad. I've copied all the playlists off his iPod onto my phone. Look. Oasis, Oasis, Oasis and Oasis. I've learned the lyrics to all their songs. I can sing like a dad. Listen."

"What?"

"I've been monitoring his conversation and his lifestyle too. So I can talk like a dad. Want to hear?"

"I already know what dads talk like. Dads say, 'What time will you be home? . . . Don't be late. . . . I'll come and pick you up.'" She turned to face me. "My dad takes an interest. He takes care of me. If I go off to some theme park, he is going to notice."

I butted in. "Ah, now, I've thought of that. I've written two letters. . . ." I got them out of my Little Stars folder to show her. "One's supposed to be from your mom to the school, saying you've got to have your appendix out. The other one—which is on proper school notepaper—is from the guidance counselor, saying you've been specially selected for a Gifted and Talented trip to the Lake District."

We were turning the corner into a little cul-de-sac. A couple of lads were playing soccer, and Ibiza was sitting on a wall. This must be Florida's house and I still hadn't persuaded her.

She was opening the door now and letting Orlando and Ibiza in. I wondered if her dad was in. But no. "He's busy," she said. "Real dads are, you know." She closed the door on me.

To be honest, this was proving harder than I'd expected. I gave it one last shot. I pushed the school letter through the letter box and shouted in after it, "Read it! It's brilliant."

✎ ✎ ✎ ✎ ✎ ✎ ✎ ✎ ✎ ✎

As you may be aware, Waterloo High has for a long time had a relationship with the South Lakeland Activity Center near Kendal. The possibility has arisen for some specially selected Year Seven pupils to attend a Gifted and Talented course at the center. Activities at the center include kayaking, abseiling, walking, pond dipping, drystone walling and nature study. Your child is one of a very few chosen for a place on this program, which will be fully funded by the Education Authority. It will be free. We strongly urge you to allow your child to benefit from this once-in-a-lifetime experience. Please sign the form below.

After a couple of minutes Florida opened the door again. I thought she'd be impressed. She said, "All this? To go on a ride?"

"Well, there's more than one ride. And the park's not in Bootle, you know. You have to get there. All the transport's sorted though. I think they're sending a limo."

"A limo? Like a real limo?"

Now she was interested.

"Yeah. A limo. You know, like a celebrity."

"Where is this theme park?"

I said, "Well, you know. It's down south. You'll need your passport for ID and stuff. You have got one, haven't you?"

I waited. Eventually she said, "I'll think about it."

I think it was good strategy to just say, "Down south," and not how far south.

I didn't say it was quite a long way south and I certainly didn't mention that it was a *really* long way east. In China.

Hello, Lucky Winners

It's no good just talking like a dad—you have to dress like one too. So on Monday night I had a look in his wardrobe. Dad wears the same jeans every day except Sunday, even though he owns four pairs. One pair was too tight on the waist. And one was from when he was trying to wear more interesting colors. They were an unusual shade of custard. They would've been a good buy for a chameleon planning to hide in a trifle. I knew Dad wouldn't miss them so I took them, along with *Talk to Your Teen*, and stuck them in the special waterproof outdoor-activities backpack Mom bought me, thinking I was going to the Lakes.

At 7:20 on Tuesday morning I texted Florida: "Limoz here." Ten minutes later she was knocking at the door.

"Where's this limo then?" she hissed. "I knew you were making it up."

"Hello, Florida," said Dad. "Are you going on this trip too then?"

"Yes, Mr. Digby."

"I'm cooking some bacon," said Dad. "D'you want a bit while you're waiting for the minibus?"

"Minibus?" said Florida, glaring at me. But just as she did, the transport arrived. It slid round the corner like a glossy shark—a long, black limo.

"Blimey!" Dad whistled. "School geography trips have changed a bit since my day."

"It's not a geography trip," said Mom. "It's for Gifted and Talented pupils. Didn't you read the letter?"

"Yeah, but . . . I just didn't know he was *that* gifted. Or that talented. And I didn't know Florida was gifted at all."

Florida snarled. Mom said, "Of course she's talented! Don't you remember? She was Sophie in *The BFG*. She remembered all her lines. What's that smell?"

"Oh," said Dad. "My bacon." And he ran back into the kitchen.

A man was getting out of the limo now and opening the back passenger door. People up and down the street were looking out of their front doors and peeping out from behind their curtains.

Florida said, "Let's go."

I said, "Yeah," and kissed my mom and shouted good-bye to Dad. Then we climbed into the back of the limo. I looked back for a second—at my mom and dad in the door-way, with bacon smoke blowing out of the door from behind them and the smoke alarm blasting away.

Mom shouted, "Look after him, Florida."

And I said, "See you." I didn't think then that maybe I wouldn't see them again. And that that would be my last sight of them. I've thought about it since though.

It wasn't some bachelorette-party stretch limo, by the way. It was a nice black Audi Quattro. There was a really polite satnav. Dad's satnav just goes, "Left . . . right . . . stop . . ." and it sounds like an alien storm trooper who has hijacked your car. This one had a flutey girl's voice and it said please and thank you.

The driver had a special cap and gray uniform. His name was Barney. There were two big paper bags on the backseat. "Goody bags," said Barney. "Just like at the Oscars, eh?"

If "limo" had a magical effect on Florida, you should have seen what "Oscars" did. Apparently when celebrities go to the Oscars or whatever, they're all given a bag full of complimentary products. Today, as Florida very quickly pointed out, we were the celebrities.

She leaned back in her seat and looked out at the streets we were leaving behind. "I wonder," she said, "what the ordinary people are doing today." Then she started rooting around in her goody bag. She found a brand-new fourth-generation Draxcommunications phone, a Draxcom watch,

Draxcom sunglasses, and a Draxcom T-shirt, a box of chocolates with the Draxcom logo on the front and a little pink Gamemaiden—which is like a girly Game Boy made by Draxcom.

I got the phone in my goody bag too. It was pretty cosmic. It had DraxWorld on it, and Draxcall—which lets you use bits of video instead of a ringtone. Florida made a video ringtone of a crowd of people in a studio, all clapping and cheering and calling her name, as though she was a guest on a chat show.

The rest of the grown-ups' goody bag was different, though. Instead of chocolate and stuff, I got a voucher for a car-hire company, a little book about golf courses, and a thing like a blue credit card that helped you work out your stress levels.

Mine said, "Relaxed."

The satnav said, "Now, as we cruise along the bypass, let's take a moment to listen to a message from your host, Dr. Drax."

Hello, lucky winners. I cannot wait to see you all at our secret headquarters and I hope you're having a comfortable journey. I ran this competition for fathers because I believe that fathers have a lot to give. My father, for instance, gave me the Drax

Communications Company. For my twelfth birthday. Bye for now. And see you at a secret location very very soon.

It turned out that even though Florida knew the name of every single person who had ever been on a reality TV show, she had never even heard of Dinah Drax.

"How can you not have heard of Dinah Drax? You've got DraxWorld on your phone."

"I didn't know Drax was a person. I thought it was just a word, like 'phone' or 'Mercedes.'"

"Mercedes *is* a person. She was the daughter of the man who owned the company."

"Never heard of her either. She's not a celebrity, is she? Otherwise she'd be in the magazines, wouldn't she?"

"Lots of people are famous who are not in your magazines."

"Like who?"

I made a list. It was completely amazing how many very famous people Florida had never heard of. For instance, Rob Pardo, Jeff Kaplan and Tom Chilton—she'd never heard of them, even though they invented World of Warcraft and revolutionized online game playing! Tolkien—cosmic author of *Lord of the Rings*? No. She got confused between Buzz Aldrin—second man on the moon—and Buzz Lightyear—a toy. She recognized Hitler's second name but she thought his first name was Heil.

Barney gave a little snort when he heard that.

Florida snapped, "Excuse me, what are you laugh . . ." but she didn't finish her sentence. She just said, "Wow!"

We had just driven into a field and there, on the grass, where you might expect to see a cow, was a big red airplane.

"That," said Florida, "is a Learjet, as flown by John Travolta."

Barney smiled. "You may not know much about world leaders of the twentieth century, but you're definitely up to date with celebrity transport."

"Whose is it?" asked Florida.

"For today," said Barney, "it's yours."

I did think that going on a plane might make Florida suspicious about just where Infinity Park was. But she was so thrilled by the celebrityness of it all that she forgot to wonder where it was going to take her. In fact, before the car had even stopped she was somehow standing on the steps of the plane. I said thank you for the lift and tried to make myself look as dadly as possible. I grabbed a newspaper out of the seat pocket and stuck it under my arm and brushed my hair forward. I definitely *felt* older.

When I got near to Florida she spread out her arms and grinned at me. I couldn't figure out what she thought she was doing but then she hissed, "Photo. Take photos. With your phone. It's what dads do."

"My dad doesn't."

"Well, mine does. He's like my own personal paparazzi."

"Paparazzo. Paparazzi is when there's more than one."

"And he doesn't correct everything I say either."

Competitive Dadliness

There was a small, neat woman waiting on the steps of the plane. She had very white teeth and her hair was as smooth and black as Playmobil. She offered Florida her hand and said, "Florida Digby! So pleased to meet you. How does it feel to have one of the four best dads in the world?"

"Who are you?" said Florida.

"I," said the woman, "am Dinah Drax."

Dr. Drax! The woman herself! When it was my turn to shake her hand I got so excited I forgot to let go of it. She must've thought I was trying to get one of her fingers as a souvenir. I tried to think of something clever to say, but all I could manage was "I love your phones."

"A lot of people do, you know. Thank goodness."

"He's always going on about you," said Florida.

"All complimentary, I hope."

"I don't know—I never listen to him. *Love* this plane."

The plane was impressive, I have to say. It didn't have rows of seats like a normal plane. It had couches and easy chairs and little tables. There were three children down at the front and Galaxy Trader playing on a big video screen. And three dads at the back, on the couches.

"Maybe Florida would like to go and play with the other children, while I introduce you to the other dads."

"Okay."

"You can let go of my hand now, Mr. Digby."

"Sorry."

I hadn't known until then that Dinah Drax was Chinese. Drax isn't her real name. Her real name means something like "Victorious Over Life's Tribulations," but she changed it to Drax because "Victorious Over Life's Tribulations" didn't fit on the side of a phone.

She took me to the back of the plane, where the dads were sitting around. One of them was a skinny man with a big fat book about prime numbers. Now I thought I knew all about prime numbers, because of being Gifted and Talented, et cetera. But what I know about them comes to about a page. This book was at least a thousand pages long, and he'd nearly finished it. So he was roughly a thousand times cleverer than me. He looked up from the book and smiled.

"I'm Samson Two's father," he said. He pointed over at

Samson Two, who was sitting next to Florida, also reading a big fat book.

"I'm Liam," I said, and before I could ask him why Samson Two had such a weird name, he said, "And my name is Samson One. I am from Waterloo," he said.

"I'm from Waterloo too," I said, "but not the one with the neighboring jungle, the one on the bypass."

He went back to reading his book.

The next dad had a bald head and a nice blue suit. He gave me a card with his name and phone number on it and pointed to a boy who was hogging the games console. "That dear, lovable boy," he said, "is my son, Hasan Xanadu. And I'm his father, Edhem. You can call me Eddie."

A man with very short hair and a big chest gave me a nod and said, "Martinet, at your service." He took my hand and gripped it so tight that I wasn't sure whether he was greeting me or trying to initiate unarmed combat. "I'm the father of Max. Max! Greet the gentleman."

At the far end of the plane a boy with exactly the same haircut as Mr. Martinet jumped up and gave me exactly the same nod. "Max is short for Maximum," said his dad, "which is what Maximum is. He's the Maximum Martinet."

"My name's Liam Digby," I said. "Please call me Liam."

He said, "Please call me Monsieur Martinet."

"Okay."

I said, "I'm Florida's father." That was the first time I'd ever said it out loud. I could feel everyone looking at me. Any minute now, I thought, one of them is going to say, "No, you're not. You're twelve." So I said the most convincingly dadly thing I could think of. I said, "Anyone watch the game last night?" They all answered at once.

"They need to buy a big defender," said Eddie Xanadu.

"The back four lack discipline," said Please-Call-Me-Monsieur Martinet.

"The laws of probability say that you can't win the Champions League just on goals. Preventing opposition goals is equally important," said Samson One.

So easy. I hadn't even seen the match!

I didn't even know if there *was* a match!

I just seemed to have a natural talent for being a grown-up.

"Well," said Dr. Drax, smiling, "I must fly! That's my little joke, by the way. I do fly the plane myself. I find it's the best way to keep our destination top secret. I'm not much of a pilot, but I'm sure I'll pick it up as we go along."

Everyone stared at her.

"Another of my little jokes!" she laughed. "Caught you all again! In fact, Daddy gave me my first flying lesson when I was still small enough to sit on his knee. I'm really rather a good pilot."

And off she went to the cockpit. I'm not sure if it's

normal for pilots to be jokey like that, but if it is, it's not a good idea. I grabbed hold of the arms of the seat, closed my eyes and tried to think of the plane as just another ride.

As rides go, the flight to China was a bit lengthy—twelve hours, I think. And once you got used to the idea that you were thirty thousand feet in the air, it wasn't that much of a thrill. But the view was pretty cosmic—miles and miles of clouds, like a country made of squirty cream. I remember watching the plane's shadow moving across the white—like a little dog running over snow.

Eddie Xanadu was sitting next to me. He said, "It's a nice plane, yes?"

"Best I've ever been in."

"My Hasan has an ambition to buy a plane like this. And he will do it. He is so good with money—even when he was very small, at his first school. In my country, things are always changing because of wars and so on. One time, the school uniform changed. First you wore a white shirt, now you must wear a blue shirt. Everyone goes to the shops to find the blue shirts. There are none. Next day Hasan comes to school and opens his bag—hundred blue shirts! He bought them all! Everyone bought a shirt from him. Just a little more expensive than the shop. So he makes money. By the time he is twelve, he had enough money to buy a house. He rents it out. Are you good with money, Mr. Digby?"

I realized I didn't actually have any money on me. I just said, "No. Not like that. Not at all."

"Hasan is a genius with money."

"Excuse me," said Samson One, "I couldn't help overhearing the conversation. Is your boy really a genius?"

"More than a genius. A wizard with money."

"Oh. With money," said Samson One, shaking his head with disappointment. "Samson Two is officially a genius. He did a project on irrigation, and it was so good the government bought it."

"How much did they pay?" asked Eddie.

"Fifty thousand dollars."

"My Hasan would've got you twice as much."

Monsieur Martinet chimed in. "Money is a terrible distraction. My Max is too focused to care about money."

"What's he focused on?" I asked, just to be polite.

"Success."

"Oh. Right."

"Are you interested in success, Mr. Digby? I have written a bestselling book on the subject. I believe everyone can be a winner. It just takes a little discipline."

My World of Warcraft guild had once taken over an entire territory. We were even going to rename it. But then it was completely destroyed by a flight of dragons. I said, "Interested but not, you know, bothered."

"What about Florida? What is her speciality? Is she a financial wizard? A natural leader? A genius?"

"You are joking." I laughed.

They all looked a bit baffled, and after a while Samson One said, "Why would that be funny?"

"All she thinks about is shopping and celebrities. All she wants is to be famous."

"How strange," said Monsieur Martinet.

"Not really. All her friends are just as bad."

"I meant, how strange for a man to talk about his own daughter in that way."

"Oh," I said. "Well . . . you know . . ."

It turns out that being a dad is a competitive sport. You're supposed to think your kid is the best kid. You're even supposed to try and convince other people that your kid is the best kid. You're supposed to be *proud* of your child.

I sneaked my dad's copy of *Talk to Your Teen* out of my waterproof backpack, but I thought the other dads might be suspicious if they caught me using the instruction manual so I took it to the loo. (Reading in the loo is definitely dadly.) It's all about listening, apparently. If you don't listen, your child becomes introverted and sulky. The more you listen, the more you'll understand. The more you understand, the more you'll find to be proud of them. And if you're proud of them, they'll be proud of themselves. Later I tried listening to Florida—she was down at the other end of the plane going on about Daytona or Paris or Britney or someone:

"You see, her mother had chronic obesity. You know what that is?"

"She was fat for a very long time?"

"And that's why she has got all these eating disorders, because she doesn't want to be like her mother. . . ." Et cetera.

It didn't seem to help. In fact, I thought it might be better if she did get a bit introverted and sulky.

Then we landed. And then the doors opened. It was dark outside but the plane soon filled up with the smell of toasted sand.

Florida said, "Are we on the beach?"

I said, "No, we're not on the beach."

"We are in the desert," said Samson Two. "And taking into account speed and direction, I would estimate that the desert in question is the Gobi. Sometimes known as Han-Hai, or the Dry Sea."

Florida said, "I didn't know we had deserts in England."

"England?" Samson Two laughed. "We're not in England. We're in China."

Florida turned on me. "CHINA! *Ohmygodwhatveyou done?* CHINA! How can we be in Chinayouidiot? I knew. I knew. I just knew you'd do something like this. Well, you can just take me home right now!"

"Home?" I said, "What d'you want me to do? Hire a cab? Give you a piggyback? Do you know how far away we are?"

"I know we're in Chinayouidiot."

Chinayouidiot was turning into a country in its own right.

Everyone was staring at her now.

"Oh dear." Dr. Drax sighed. "We girls are so complicated. Let's leave Dad to sort this out, shall we? I imagine Mr. Digby knows how to deal with his own daughter."

I don't know what made her imagine that. Florida was actually kicking me now and bawling, "You said we were going to a theme park!"

"We are. This is it."

"It's in the desert. Not even a normal desert. A Chinese desert. In China. You said it was down south."

"It is down south."

"I thought you meant London."

"But we were on a plane for hours. If you're on a plane

for hours and hours, obviously you're going to go farther than London."

"I thought it was a slow plane."

A slow plane.

Don't be afraid of temper tantrums. Often teens will have something they need to tell you but which they find difficult to say. Anger helps them say it. Think of the anger as emotional FedEx—something you turn to when the normal post just isn't fast enough.

from Talk to Your Teen

Talk to Your Teen does not have a chapter specifically called "When Daughters Kick You in Public." In fact, when it came to Florida, World of Warcraft was more useful. You just had to think of her as a kind of monster and remember that every monster has a soft zone.

I'd already identified Florida's. So when I noticed that the others were all shuffling around on the steps of the plane, arranging themselves into some kind of group, I pretended to ignore Florida and shouted like I was talking to Dr. Drax, "It's okay, Dr. Drax. Florida doesn't want to be in the group photograph."

As soon as she heard the word "photograph," Florida sat up and started listening. I said, "It's just a group photo.

For the newspapers or something. I'm not sure. Don't worry about it. You just keep kicking me."

"Newspapers?"

"Or magazines. I didn't hear which. Oh, maybe it's for TV. Honestly, kick away."

Florida was doing one of her smiles in the front row of that photograph before I had time to stand up. Dr. Drax said, "Well, Mr. Digby, you certainly seem to be a very effective parent. Smile for the camera, everyone."

In Chinayouidiot

"We have reached our destination," said Dr. Drax. "Welcome to Infinity Park. It's too dark now to see it properly and you'll be too tired to appreciate it."

A thing like a minibus with Caterpillar tracks came to take us to our accommodation. I remember looking out of the window but there was nothing to see—just the odd campfire and every now and then a car.

We'd been driving for about ten minutes when the minibus thing stopped suddenly and Dr. Drax asked us to look out of the windows on the left side of the bus. At first there was nothing but darkness, but then suddenly something like a massive door had opened. There was a building. It looked like a big red cliff lit by banks and banks of spotlights. It was bigger than the biggest skyscraper you've ever seen, and had massive Chinese letters painted down the side.

"What is it?" said, well, everyone really.

"That," said Dr. Drax, "is the Possibility Building."

"But what's inside?"

"Inside there is our main attraction. Inside there is the Rocket."

"But what is the Rocket? What kind of ride is it? What's it like?"

"What's it like? It's not like anything. It's unique. It is the biggest thrill ride in the history of the world, that's all. I can't describe it because it's indescribable."

When I was being a grown-up in Liverpool, I got free yogurt. In China I got My Own House! The minibus thing dropped us off at a little cluster of bungalows with lawns and street-lights and traffic islands, like a housing development.

A whole bungalow all to ourselves. I said to Florida, "Isn't this brilliant?"

"Basically you've kidnapped me and taken me to a desert, a desert in China."

"I suppose. But come on—apart from the fact that it's in China—what d'you think? I mean, look at this house!"

"There's nothing *apart from* being in China, Liam. Being in China is major."

The house was mostly one big open room—with a kitcheny bit at one end and two huge couches at the other and a weird kind of little garden full of cacti in between.

"And," said Florida, looking all around it, "it's got no TV."

"Well, maybe we could ask for a TV. Anyway, it's probably good that we haven't got one because we're supposed to get up early in the . . ."

Florida had found a little panel of buttons in the arm of the couch. When she touched one, the whole living room wall turned blue and started to hum, and then a picture appeared with sound. The television was an entire wall of the living room.

"Now this," said Florida, "is good."

We both flopped onto the couch. We were hypnotized. It was amazing even when it was only showing farming news in Cantonese, but after a bit of channel flicking we found an American channel that was showing *Celebrity Séance* (where living celebrities try to contact the spirits of dead celebrities) and Florida looked like she'd gone to heaven.

"Look!" she yelled. "There's Lindsey. Aaaah!" Lindsey was the presenter, but Florida acted like Lindsey was like her mom, her sister, her cat and her favorite blanket all rolled into one.

I said, "As soon as this is finished, lights out and bed. Big day tomorrow."

"Liam, stop talking like a grown-up. There's no grown-up

here—that's the only good thing about it."

"But I'm supposed to be your dad. That's the whole point. I've got to act the role of your dad. So I'm getting into character, like Lisa said."

"If you're going to be a dad, be like my dad, not like yours. Get me presents, and ice cream; don't sit there telling me about history and stuff."

"D'you know what time it is? Isn't it a bit late for ice cream?"

"It would be if you were a real dad. But you're not. You're a kid. I'm a kid. We can do what we want. If we want ice cream for supper, we can have ice cream for supper."

And apparently we did want ice cream for supper. Luckily there were *buckets* of ice cream, including Chocapocalypse flavor, in the freezer.

Florida took it back to the couch and sat there in front of the TV. Every few seconds, she'd poke her spoon in. "And if we want to watch TV all night," she said, "we can."

"Yeah, but—"

"Not 'Yeah, but.' Just 'Yeah.'"

While she was busy with the ice cream, I sneaked another look at *Talk to Your Teen* and found a bit about how to lay down ground rules and make sure your teen has barriers. I was just going to set a few barriers in place when Florida yelled, "Liam! Come and look at this!"

She'd discovered that you could send pictures from her Draxphone to the big screen. She made me video her doing an acceptance speech and then project it onto the wall.

"I want to thank my mom and especially my dad. I hope you're proud of your little princess now," she said. "And I hope together we can end global warming and poverty and stuff."

It looked wobbly but convincing on the big screen. I said, "What exactly are you accepting?"

"An award."

"For what?"

"For being famous."

I went to get a drink out of the fridge and found some little bottles of water shaped like rockets, with fins and a pointy bit at the top. They were perfect weapons for a water fight. I stuffed three in each pocket, tiptoed back to the living room and squirted Florida. She shrieked and ran after me. I threw her a bottle just to make it fair and we had this excellent water fight all over the house. I hid behind the couch, hoping to ambush her. I must've fallen asleep there, because the next thing I knew, the phone was ringing.

"This is your alarm call," it said. "Please join your party in the car park of the Possibility Building at eight a.m."

I picked my way through the discarded ice-cream buckets and over the soaking wet floors and eventually found

Florida curled up asleep in the cupboard with the cleaning stuff. I woke her up (she wasn't happy) and went to get changed.

I emptied my bag onto my bed so that I could sort everything out. There were some Warcraft notes, and an unexpected envelope, which turned out to contain a photograph of me, Mom and Dad on my First Communion day—Mom must have sneaked it in there. Dad's broken St. Christopher statue was at the bottom of the bag too. He must've sneaked that in too. He'd obviously been worried about me going to the Lake District on my own. I've brought it with me into space. It's standing on top of the multifunctional display, just like it used to stand on the dashboard of his taxi. If my dad could see it now, he'd be *really* worried.

Thrill Ride of the Century

This part of space seems to be a communications dead zone. I can't get any signal on my phone. Maybe we're on the wrong side of the satellites. I'm going through old messages in my in-box for company. I've still got the last one Dr. Drax sent: "Tk care of u-self & children. C u in 10 hrs." That was about twenty-four hours ago. Not only have I not seen Dr. Drax, I haven't seen her planet.

I've also still got the first one. It says: "Welcum 2 Infinity Park. B @ Poss Blding car park @ 8. Courtesy car in drive. Use phone to open car. Drv safely."

Courtesy car!

"What's a courtesy car?" said Florida.

"Well, it's a car that they lend you and you can use it as much as you like."

"You mean a car for you to drive? Oh no, no, no, no, no,

no, no! Not after last time," said Florida. Then she said, "What kind of car is it? Is it another limo?"

"Let's go and see."

It was a little greeny Toyota-y thing. It looked like a big toy really. I put my hand out to touch it.

"Liam. . . ," said Florida. "We can't."

"No, we can't. You're right. Except . . ."

"Except what?"

"Except I am supposed to be a taxi driver."

"Oh."

"So I've got to pretend I can drive."

"Liam, you can only pretend you can drive in a pretend car. In a real car, you have a real accident and get us really killed."

"It doesn't look that dangerous. I mean, it looks a lot less dangerous than the Porsche did. The text said you open it with your phone."

I pointed the phone at it and the headlights blinked and all the doors popped open. Then a robot-y voice from the dashboard said, "Climb aboard, Liam Digby." You have to admit this was interesting. You can't really blame us for getting inside the car. It would've been rude not to.

As soon as we were in the seats, the car spoke again. "Hi, Liam, hi, Florida," it said. "This drive should take fifteen minutes. Don't forget to fasten your seat belts." And, without us doing anything, the engine started up. A nice, gentle little engine. It sounded so reassuring. It sounded like it *trusted* us. We fastened our seat belts.

Florida was looking around the inside of the car. "There's something missing," she said. "It's got hardly any levers or buttons."

"It's an automatic. My dad drove one once when he was covering for someone else. He said it was like driving a bumper car."

Florida said, "Bumper cars are easy to drive."

It was hard to disagree with this. I've driven loads of bumper cars. Not one of them stretched my abilities. And this car seemed so helpful.

While I was trying to come to a decision I touched one of the buttons on the dashboard. Florida yelped, "Don't! It could be the ejector seat or something!"

The windshield wipers started banging over and back across the windshield. We both laughed. At least we knew what one of the levers was for. And the one with the picture of the headlight on was probably the headlights, so the one with the numbers on must be the one to make it go. I pushed it down one notch very gently and the noise in the engine changed to an angry roar. And the satnav said, "That's my accelerator. Don't forget my handbrake."

It wasn't even me. It was Florida who found the handbrake and slipped it. The car rolled forward, purring. Suddenly there was a different noise—a big honking noise, and some squealing and lights flashing. Another car was driving up behind us when we pulled out. Other cars! I'd forgotten about other cars. This one swerved out past us and honked us again. Another one squealed and honked just behind us.

"This is brilliant!" whooped Florida inexplicably.

The hardest part about driving a car is keeping it in the right place on the road. You mustn't go too near the curb (your tires make a weird screaming noise) or too far over to the middle (drivers coming the other way look frightened and angry).

At first I tried to stay pretty much in the middle. When I looked in my rearview mirror there was a line of cars behind me doing exactly the same, so it must've been right. There was nothing at all ahead of us.

"Kings of the road!" yelled Florida.

We did everything the satnav told us and soon, instead of driving past neat lawns and white bungalows, we were bumping along a narrow cinder track through a field full of tents and huts. Little kids kept running up to the car, banging on the window and smiling at us. There were donkeys and ponies tied up at the side of the road. A camel even walked in front of us. I said, "This can't be right."

But the satnav said, "Yes, this is right. Stop worrying." Now that's what I call an impressive level of interactivity.

Then we saw it. Beyond the tents and over to the left, the Possibility Building. It really was big. And red. Like a huge unopened present. I was trying to imagine what was inside, which is probably why the car drifted slightly off the side of the track, which is probably what led to the sirens and flashing lights going off all over the place and Florida shouting, "Stop! Stop!" I did stop. I stopped surprisingly completely. When we looked up there were two policemen coming toward us with guns.

"Well, game over," said Florida. "They are going to ask to see your license. They'll find out you're not a grown-up and they'll send us home."

Her theory was much more optimistic than mine. My theory was that they were going to shoot us.

The police in fact bowed to us, got on their radios, talked in Chinese for a while, then bowed again and one of them said, "Honored guests?" in English.

"Yes," said Florida, "honored guests. That's us."

Then he did this mime which I think meant, Follow-us-in-your-car-even-though-you-blatantly-can't-drive. And they led us all the way to the Possibility Building car park. This was the best thing ever according to Florida, because it was a police escort and even Madonna doesn't get a police escort.

"That's because Madonna doesn't have a dad like yours," I said.

Dr. Drax was waiting for us with the other kids and dads. She asked if we were ready to see the biggest thrill ride in the world ever.

I said, "Yes!" slightly too loud and too excited to be truly dadly.

"Then let's go," said Dr. Drax.

The Possibility Building is so big that sometimes there are proper rain clouds floating around inside it. A room with its own weather. I can tell you all that now. But I didn't notice any of this at the time. I didn't notice it because I was too busy looking at Infinity Park's main attraction, the World's Biggest Thrill Ride, the ride I'd been waiting to see all this time: the Rocket. In front of me. And above me. Way, way, way above me. Because the Rocket goes all the way past the interior clouds, to the roof.

And the reason this ride is called the Rocket is that it is a rocket.

A real rocket.

A blue rocket.

A massive rocket.

Of the going-to-space kind.

It was so massive that at first we couldn't tell it *was* a rocket. It looked like a wall of metal pipes and panels. We couldn't take it in. We all looked up and then looked down, as though we were a bunch of scanners trying to upload an image. Samson Two seemed to have the fastest processor. "It's a rocket," he said.

"Yes." Dr. Drax smiled. "It's my rocket."

How good is that sentence? "It's my rocket," like "It's my lunch box," or something.

"Of course we have been making rockets here in China since Feng Jishen invented the first one in the year 970 AD. At first they were used to fire arrows. They had names like *Swarm of Bees* or *Five Leaping Tigers*. But my rocket has a different purpose. It's called the *Infinite Possibility*. And . . ." she said, turning to the kids, "I'm giving it to you. I'd like you children to think of it as a present. From my generation to yours. I'm not going to ride in it. But you are."

"When you say ride in it," said Samson One, "do you mean, ride in it . . . to space?"

"Yes. The biggest thrill ride of all time is a ride to space. I'm sorry to have been so secretive about this. It was only because . . . it's a secret. And we want to keep it that way. Any questions?"

Monsieur Martinet said, "You want to send our children to space?"

"For just a few hours. The rocket will pop up to space, do

a simple little job and then pop down again." She made it sound like an elevator. "As thrill rides go, it's the ultimate."

Everyone agreed.

Dr. Drax went on, "Most thrill rides have a height requirement. This one will need a bit more—you'll have to pass some medicals and you'll need to train."

"We're going to be astronauts," said Samson Two.

"In fact, here in China the word is 'taikonaut.' Yes, you are all going to be taikonauts, with parental permission, of course."

All the kids looked round at their dads for permission. I even looked round for mine. Then I remembered that mine wasn't there. I was the dad this time.

Dr. Drax turned to the children again and said, "I called the rocket a present, but it's more a kind of apology. You see, I believe my generation has all but destroyed this pretty blue planet. I hope I'm wrong, but if I'm not then the only hope for humankind might be for us to start again somewhere else. Just because we've destroyed the Earth, that doesn't mean it's the end of the world. There are millions and millions of stars in the universe. There are probably even millions of planets like this one. Every bit as good as this one. It's just a matter of finding one.

"If we're going to do that, we are going to have to make some long journeys, journeys that might take years. And if a journey is going to take years, you'd better have a young crew. So that they'll still be strong and useful when they arrive. And that is what Infinity Park is all about. I want it to be a place that will inspire young people like you to want to work in space. In fact, if they come to the park, some of them will be able to go to space, just for a little while. This is the prototype. You will be the first. The first children in space." Then she said, "Any questions?"

Florida's hand shot up. "Does that mean we're going to be famous?" she said.

"Maybe. But not yet. As I said, this mission is a secret—our little secret."

"How famous?"

"Well . . . world famous, I suppose. Maybe. As long as everything goes to plan."

Florida was bouncing on the balls of her feet with sheer happiness. She put her hand up again.

"Florida?"

"I love this color," said Florida, pointing at the rocket. "What do you call it?"

"I call it blue," said Dr. Drax. "I think most people do."

"But there's blue and blue. This is a lovely shade."

"Perhaps we could call it Rocket Blue. Next question?"

The next question was from Samson Two. "Could we call it Ballistic Blue? Ballistics is the science of rockets, and Ballistic Blue has a nice alliterative quality."

"Very nice," smiled Dr. Drax. "Next question?"

Hasan said, "That's a lot of paint. Did the supplier offer you a good discount for placing such a large order?"

"Does anyone have any questions that are not about the paintwork?" said Dr. Drax.

No one did. "In that case, one of our engineers will now show the children around the rocket while we grown-ups get down to the paperwork. Rather a lot of forms to fill in for this trip, I'm afraid. Surprisingly difficult to get insured for a flight into space. Even though this one is extremely safe. Completely safe. Almost."

You could see that Dr. Drax was disappointed, that she thought the children had sort of missed the point, going on about the paint like that. But that's what kids do when big things come up. We focus on the little things. Like the kids sleeping in this rocket now. They're not dreaming about planet Earth. They're dreaming about their own little bedrooms.

I had a different reaction to the rocket. I wasn't interested in the paint. I had one thought. One big, damp thought. Namely:

I AM NOT GOING TO SPACE.

The children are having the thrill ride of the century. And we—the grown-ups—are going to sit around and watch and maybe video them or something.

"Come along, children," smiled Dr. Drax as the kids all climbed on to the escalator platform at the side of the rocket.

I said, "But we can see round the rocket too, can't we?"

"I'm afraid not," Dr. Drax smiled. "I want the children to get used to being together without their daddies. After all, they won't have their daddies in space."

That's right.

Because . . .

I am not going to space.

Florida Kirby *is* going to space.

That is exactly the wrong way round. It's supposed to be *more* fun being a grown-up. That's why I swapped being a kid for being a dad. What's the *point* in forfeiting your childhood if all you get for it is filling in forms?

I Am the Space Daddy

When I realized I'd gone all the way to the Gobi Desert just to watch Florida Kirby going to space I felt like I'd died. Not died as in real life. But died as in a game—when you're running along nicely on Level Forty, having all sorts of Level Forty–type adventures, and *bleep*, you're dead with no spare lives, and you have to go right back to the beginning, and go through all the boring bits all over again.

While Florida and the other kids were looking around a real rocket, we dads had to sit down and fill in forms. Forms full of questions about our children. I can't believe how much parents are supposed to know about their kids. Like their date of birth, for instance. In fact I was all right with that one because I still had Florida's passport so I just copied her birthday out of that.

"Oh dear," said Dr. Drax. "Here's a daddy who doesn't

know his own daughter's birthday."

"I know Samson Two's birthday," said Samson One, "and one day the world will know it too. It will be a national holiday in our country."

"I do sometimes forget Max's," said Monsieur Martinet, "but he is too well brought up to say so."

The birthday question turned out to be the easy one. There were questions about vaccinations, allergies and what childhood illnesses she'd had. I did remember that she'd been off school a lot in Year Six, but I couldn't remember why.

All the other dads were ticking things off and filling things in. I tried to see what Max's dad was writing so I could copy, but he caught me looking and put his hand over his forms so I couldn't see. Childhood illnesses. I couldn't think of one childhood illness. Except that when Florida was talking about celebrities earlier she'd mentioned chronic something. I thought if I wrote "chronic" it would help me remember the other word. That was it—chronic obesity.

Dr. Drax was looking over my shoulder. She said, "Chronic obesity? Are you sure?"

Then luckily I remembered that "obesity" means "fat." I said, "Not chronic obesity, sorry." I crossed out "obesity" and put "arthritis." It looked quite convincing written down.

Dr. Drax sniffed quite hard, then took the form off me and looked at it. "I see under vaccinations, you've ticked yellow fever and malaria."

I'd ticked quite a few to be on the safe side.

"Oh, and dengue fever. Has Florida traveled a lot?"

"Yes, I think so."

"Think so?"

"I mean, I think she has because she has. She's been to Florida. Hence the name. And . . . we all went to Enchantment Land in Southport in Year Six. I mean, when *she* was in Year Six."

"Southport in England?"

"Yes."

"Only you don't normally need vaccinations if you're traveling within England."

"Not normally, no," I said. "But I say . . . why take the risk? You can't be too careful—that's the Digby family motto."

After the paperwork, it got worse. We played golf.

Golf! The other dads couldn't have been more excited if you'd given them invisibility cloaks.

Golf while Florida was looking around a rocket.

Golf while she was getting ready to be a taikonaut.

Golf.

Golf. If you think Monopoly is boring, you should try golf. If you were playing golf inside World of Warcraft, what skills would you need? Running skills? No. Sword skills?

No. Cunning? No. Wisdom? You are joking. The object of the "game" is to put a ball in a hole. Tidying-up skills, that's what you'd need. Tidying-up skills and a lot of time on your hands. A game? I suppose it feels like a game if you are actually one of the undead.

We pootled around this golf course in two electric buggies while they all talked about their averages and handicaps, and told stories about times when they'd put other little balls in different little holes.

"I taught Samson Two to play golf some years ago," said Samson One as we lined up to take our first shots. "Such a practical way to learn about the interaction of physical forces and so on. For instance, if I use a driver to tee off . . ." A driver is one of those golf sticks for hitting the ball with—apparently they've got different names, like wedge and iron and stuff. Anyway, Samson One teed off with a driver and explained about how the parabola of the ball in flight was related to the swing of the driver as he hit the ball—I wasn't really listening. I just hit the ball as hard as I could. It flew down the grass. I shouted, "Yes!!!!"

The others just stared at me, and Monsieur Martinet said, "Why are you so happy?"

"I hit it loads farther than him. I'm winning."

Samson One laughed. "But you've hit it too far. It's gone past the hole and into the rough."

I had sort of assumed that the point of the game was to hit the ball as far as you could. I hadn't known about the holes.

"Extraordinary," said Monsieur Martinet, "that one could reach adulthood without knowing how golf is played."

I said, "Yeah, but do you know how World of Warcraft is played? I bet you don't."

Monsieur Martinet sort of squinted, then said, "Golf is a game that teaches many of the qualities needed for success—for instance, decision making and attention to detail. Computer games, on the contrary, are for idiots."

"Or teenagers," said Eddie Xanadu.

I realized I'd said the wrong thing. I tried to recover a bit of ground by saying, "Let's see if you do better then." I'm not sure how dadly that sounded, to be honest.

The others all got their ball onto the flat bit of grass round the hole. I had to get mine out of the long grass. Dr. Drax came with me and told me I should chip the ball with a niblick. I was quite excited by that suggestion. I thought a niblick might be some slim pond-dwelling goblin, which is what it sounds like. Disappointingly, it's just another golf stick.

It does work though. It knocked the ball straight up into the air and it plopped down on the green bit. "Well done," said Dr. Drax. "There's no feeling on Earth as satisfying as dropping the ball down just so like that."

"Maybe not on Earth. I bet there are some much better feelings in space though."

"Yes," she said. "You've certainly given your daughter a great opportunity."

Yes, I've given Florida a great opportunity. And I've given myself a niblick.

The other dads were all lined up ready to tee off again. Samson One drove his ball down the fairway in another lovely parabola. I kept hold of my niblick.

"Oh, you can't tee off with a niblick," smiled Dr. Drax.

"I'm not teeing off." I chipped the ball into the back of the golf buggy.

"Now look what you've done," snarled Monsieur Martinet.

"I've done," I said, "a stroke of genius. When you drive up onto the green in the buggy, my ball will go to the green in the back of the buggy. And I'll just chip it out again."

"You can't do that! You can't send your ball round the golf course in a car."

"Why not?"

"The rules. Golf has rules. Lots of rules. That's the beauty of the game."

Samson One said, "Logic says he can. If we think of the

golf buggy as a hazard? Well then, balls do go into hazards. Sand traps and ponds and so on."

When you say "hazard" to normal people they think of ice on the road, or fog, or sudden invasions of Night Elves. Golfers think you mean sand. Or a puddle with a duck in it.

"Hazards," said Monsieur Martinet, "do not get up and take the balls right up to the hole, do they?"

"No. But you can't interfere with a hazard. And if this hazard happens to be heading to the green, then the ball will have to go with it."

You could tell that Monsieur Martinet was unhappy about this by the way he started waving his five iron round his head and yelling about how childish I was.

"*I'm* childish?! I'm not the one getting all stressed out about a game." Honestly, grown-ups talk about teenagers spending too much time online and taking games too seriously. A game of golf seems to take about three years, and they talk about it like the next stroke is going to save the world.

"Yes, childish. What kind of father are you? No wonder your daughter is so complicated when you have so little regard for rules!"

I looked at him. He really thought he was a Level Forty monster and I was some sort of Level Seven baby warrior who'd run away if he snarled at me. But I had my mental elixir. I let it fill my brain and then I Engaged. "You think you're a good dad? What kind of parent lets his child go off into space while he plays golf?"

Monsieur Martinet looked a bit confused when I said that. And so did the other dads. Until Dr. Drax said, "Aren't you doing exactly that, Mr. Digby?"

Well, yes, I was but I knew that my dad would never do that. Let alone my mom. I said, "In my school—my child's school—when they go on a trip, a responsible parent goes with them. Even if it's only to the museum or the art gallery. In the New Strand Shopping Center, you're not even allowed to go into the candy shop without an accompanying adult. Why aren't you doing that here?"

"You mean you'd like to go to space with the children?" asked Dr. Drax.

"Yes. Yes, of course I would!"

"But . . ."

They were all staring at me. Monsieur Martinet rolled his eyes and muttered, "Of course he should be with the children. He *is* a child. Tall, but a child."

Dr. Drax held her hands up. "I think," she said, "I am having one of my great ideas."

We waited to see what it was.

"A daddy in space. I will send one of you to space. But which one?"

I said, "Me. I'll go."

"Don't be ridiculous," snarled Monsieur Martinet. "The job needs a real leader. I'll go."

"It might be better to have someone capable of understanding the science," said Samson One. "Someone like me."

"Let's have a little competition," said Dr. Drax. "I can see from the way you play golf that you're all very competitive. And you are all so different. Monsieur Martinet imposes a strong discipline, Samson One believes in education—"

"I certainly do."

"Mr. Xanadu is very indulgent—or generous. And Mr. Digby is . . ." She looked at me as though she was trying to remember why she specially selected me. In the end she said, "Mr. Digby is available."

"When you say competition . . . ?" said Mr. Xanadu.

"Simple. You'll all do the space training with your children, and the one who proves to be the best taikonaut . . . no, not the best taikonaut, the best father—he will go to space."

Yes! I'd really leveled up this time. It was like when you get to the next stage of a game and the whole landscape changes—and it's full of new dangers and different thrills. I'd leveled up from a round of golf to space exploration.

"I will be the winner," said Monsieur Martinet. "When it comes to winning, I wrote the manual."

"Me," said Samson One. "I have the brains."

"Me," said Mr. Xanadu. "Because I want to and I do tend to get what I want."

"That," said Dr. Drax, "is for the children to decide. We'll let them vote."

I didn't say anything. I knew it was going to be me.

I was dying to hear all about the rocket. The minute Florida came through the door I said, "So what was it like? The rocket?"

She said, "'S'all right."

"That's it? Your first day on a real rocket and that's all you can say? ''S'all right'?"

"No."

"What else?"

"I'm starving."

I remembered the bit in *Talk to Your Teen* about using fiddly food to get teenagers to talk. I made a stir-fry and said, "Let's use real chopsticks."

"I don't know how to use chopsticks."

"There's instructions on the packet."

"They're in Chinese."

"Just try."

It made the meal last a long time, but it didn't improve the conversation because we were concentrating so hard on the chopsticks. In the end I just said, "Well, it doesn't matter if you don't tell me what the rocket's like anyway. Because I'm going on it too," and I told her all about the competition.

Finally Florida began to communicate. She said, "Hahahahahahahahahahahahahahaha."

"What's so funny?"

"Your joke. You are joking, aren't you? You don't really think you're going to win."

"I might."

"Liam, have you got a bike?"

"I've got a Cherokee Chief."

"Is it a fast bike?"

"It's got twenty-three gears."

"Could it win the Grand National?"

"No."

"Why not?"

"Because it's not a horse."

"And you won't win the dad competition because you're NOT A DAD."

"True. On the other hand, I'm not an actual elf warrior either, but the Wanderlust Warriors rule the floor in World of Warcraft."

"Liam, I have no idea what you're talking about."

"I'm saying . . . pretending sometimes works. Like at Little Stars."

"Okay . . ."

"So help me pretend to be your dad. All you have to do is call me Dad."

"Okay. I'll call you Dad . . ."

"Thanks."

". . . provided you call me your little princess."

"My little *what*?!"

"It's what my real dad calls me. I miss being called Princess. Please."

"I'll try."

The Ice-Cream Man of the Gobi Desert

My first day of taikonaut training, we had to be at the launch site before dawn. I was really excited. Florida was really sleepy. It was so dark we couldn't tell who else was there. There was just a bunch of yawning, stretching shadows. Even the Possibility Building didn't look that solid, until the sun rolled up and peeled a strip of shadow off its back, as though it was a huge red banana. And then it tore up all the other shadows like tissue paper and there was everyone unwrapped on the tarmac, like surprises.

Hasan and his father were sitting in a golf buggy. "I enjoy riding in it so much," said Eddie, "I decide to buy one for my dear Hasan." Hasan was at the controls. He kept driving it round in little circles to amuse himself. "Enough," said Eddie. "You make my head spin."

Monsieur Martinet was wearing a T-shirt that said "Vote Martinet." I think Samson One saw me looking at it, because he smiled at me and then rolled his eyes. I've seen other dads do this to my dad sometimes when we're out shopping with Mom. It's like a secret dad sign or something. For a second I felt truly dadly so I rolled my eyes right back at him.

Then Dr. Drax arrived. "Sorry to drag you all out so early," she said. "Today is your first day as trainee taikonauts, and we're going to begin with a nice, gentle exercise in team building, problem solving and decision making. Very easy. Follow me, please."

Eddie offered her a lift in the back of his new golf buggy. She said, "How kind," and they all trundled off round the far side of the building. The rest of us tried to keep up on foot.

When we caught up with them, Dr. Drax was pointing out into the desert. "Look," she said. "The shadow of the Possibility." The building's shadow stretched out into the desert, long and straight like a road made of ink. "A road that is pointing to something. Something I'd like you all to go and find and bring back for me."

"What kind of thing?" asked Samson Two.

"Oh, nothing much. A flag. Just an ordinary little flag. It should be easy enough to spot. There's nothing else out there. All you have to do is follow the shadow."

Everyone stared out into the desert. There really wasn't

anything out there. Except geology. Miles and miles and miles of wind erosion and salt deposits.

"Hasan would like to use his new golf buggy, if you don't mind," said Eddie.

Dr. Drax laughed and explained that this wouldn't be possible. "It's not a race. I want you all to stick together. And work as a team. I've got you a little present to help you along. . . ." I thought she was going to cough up at least a jeep, and maybe some weaponry. But no. She handed Please-Call-Me-Monsieur Martinet something that looked like a massive firework. "This," she said, "is a distress flare. If you set it off we will see it, no matter how far away you are. And we'll come and get you right away. We don't want you to come to any harm."

"Thank you," said Monsieur Martinet. "I will use it wisely."

"Of course, if you do set this off, that will mean you have failed in your mission. And I'll have to find myself a brand-new crew. So if you use the flare, you lose the rocket. All righty?"

I just could not wait to walk off into the desert. The others weren't so keen. Samson One wanted to go and get protective clothing, water, sunblock, hats.

"And what if it takes longer than a day?" said Eddie.

"Maybe we should get tents. And tinned food. And plates. Because when you eat on the beach, sand gets into your food. It must be even worse in the desert."

"This is turning into a shopping trip!" said Florida. "I love it!"

I said, "Can't we just go *now*?!" and realized straight-away that this lacked dadliness so I said, "I have actually organized desert expeditions before so I know a bit about it. And in my experience, the sooner you set off the better."

Everyone stared at me. "You've organized a desert expedition before?" said Monsieur Martinet. "I thought you were a taxi driver before."

"This was before before, before I was a taxi driver."

"You never told me that before, Daddy," said Florida with a big phony smile. "A desert expedition? Honest?"

"Yeah. So . . . let's go."

"I really think we ought to prepare," said Samson One.

"In fact," said Samson Two, "Mr. Digby may have a point. The only clue we have about the location of the flag is that it lies somewhere on the line of the building's shadow. At the moment—just after dawn—the shadow is at its longest. As the day goes on, the shadow will get shorter. We'll have less shade. And less information."

"That," I said, "is completely what I was saying. Let's go!"

* * *

Inside the shadow it was surprisingly cool. Florida padded along next to me, going on about how she'd been promised a thrill ride. "This is not a ride," she said. "This is a punishment."

"Florida, it's Friday morning, you're supposed to be in double math. Instead you're walking in the Gobi Desert."

"Which you've done before, apparently."

"I didn't say I'd walked in this desert. I said I'd led an expedition across a desert. And I have."

"What desert was it then? The Bootle Desert?"

"It was the Blasted Lands of Azeroth, actually. And it was a lot worse than this. It had giant insects, for one thing. And a portal to the evil netherlands."

"Liam, what are you talking about?"

"Don't call me Liam, and I'm talking about World of Warcraft."

"Well, don't talk about it anymore. Dads don't. And why, by the way, are we walking in the shadow? We could be getting a tan." As she said it she stepped out of the shadow and into the sun. From where I was standing it looked like she'd vanished completely. Then she bounced back into the shade really quickly.

"Ow, ow, do you even *know* how hot it is out there? We're going to be cooked."

"That's why we've got to try and do this before we lose the shade."

"And why is it so *sandy*?!" She seemed to think the Gobi Desert was my fault.

"Because the area in which we are standing was once the seabed of a great ocean that was exposed to the wind by a fall in the water level. The rocks and the mountains that were on the seabed have been broken down into sand by the wind over the last thousand million years."

"Liam, I don't *care*!!!"

She shouted so loud that you could hear her words moving away from us over the dunes. Then we heard something that sounded like God hoovering the world. It was the wind. A wind that threw sand at our legs and arms so hard it felt like we were being stabbed with a billion nano-knives. Sand went into your mouth and up your nostrils and, worst of all, in your eyes. We all got into a kind of scrum, with our backs to the desert and our heads in a circle. Monsieur Martinet's face was right in my face. He snarled, "Well, Mr. Digby, you've done this before. What do you suggest we do now?"

I said, "Wait for the wind to die down?"

"You'll be waiting a long time," said Florida. "It's been blowing for a thousand million years so far, apparently."

I hadn't thought of that. I felt weirdly impressed with her.

I said, "That's an amazing thought, Florida."

"Oh," said Florida. "Thanks, Liam."

I pinched her and she said, "Dad, I mean. Not Liam." Then she put her sunglasses on and said, "Oh, that's much better." No one else put theirs on, but everyone stared at her. "Has no one else brought their sunglasses?"

"It was dark," said Samson Two. "It seemed unnecessary."

"I just thought they looked cool," explained Florida. "David Beckham wears sunglasses in the dark."

"Dad," said Hasan, "she's got sunglasses. I want them."

"Of course," said Eddie. "Little girl, how much for the sunglasses?"

"I'm not selling them."

"Mr. Digby, how much for your daughter's sunglasses? We would like to buy them."

"They're not mine. They're hers."

"But she's your daughter. You tell her to sell them."

"I won't," I said, "but I do have a plan. My daughter was the only one sensible enough to bring sunglasses, right? So this is what we do. She wears her glasses. The rest of us cover our faces with our T-shirt or whatever and hold hands in a line, and she goes at the front and leads us to the flag."

They were all quiet for a moment and then Samson One said, "That's actually a good plan."

"I used it last time I was in the desert," I said. Which was true. I used it to get a bunch of Night Elves out of the Labyrinth of Light.

Monsieur Martinet said it was a good idea too, but he wanted Max to be the one with the glasses, "Because Max is a natural leader."

"Maybe so," said Florida, "but the thing is, they're my glasses. Let's go."

So we set off in this conga line across the desert, while Monsieur Martinet shouted encouraging words about other people who had crossed deserts. "Mark Antony," he said, "and Lawrence of Arabia—they were humans. We are humans. Humans can do this."

It takes concentration to keep walking forward over soft sand when you're blindfolded, so nobody spoke for a while, but there was a moment when everyone stopped and thought the same thing. It was the moment when we stepped out of the shadow. You didn't need to wonder what had happened. It was like someone had pointed a flamethrower at us. I remembered that Lawrence of Arabia and Mark Antony had walked across deserts with great big armies, not with a couple of kids and their dads. And also that, by the time they finished, their armies were a lot smaller.

And then the wind dropped. And at last we could

open our eyes and see where we were. And that was bad news too.

We were standing at the bottom of a massive sand dune. A hundred-foot hill of slippy sand. You could see the wind stripping streamers of sand from the top of it. When Hasan saw the dune he started crying. "Do we have to go up there? I can't go up there. It's too high."

Monsieur Martinet seemed to see this as a challenge. But not for him. For Max. "Max," he barked, "run up the dune and see if you can see the flag."

Max looked shocked. "Why me?"

"Max," yelled Monsieur Martinet, "winners lead from the front."

"But—" said Max.

"DO AS I SAY! THIS IS A QUESTION OF DISCIPLINE!"

And Max set off up the dune, all on his own, looking really, really miserable in the soft sand.

Hasan Xanadu sat down. "I'm not going up that," he said. "Even if there are a thousand flags on the other side."

Eddie said, "My dear Hasan doesn't want to climb it. We must go round."

Samson Two thought this was not a good idea. "Dr. Drax told us to follow the line of the shadow. If we veer off we might never find it again. This is a wind-drift dune. Such dunes can be many miles long—perhaps twenty or even thirty."

Twenty or thirty miles sounded bad. But climbing that dune looked impossible.

Max was up to his knees in sand. "I can't do it," he yelled. He sounded like he was going to cry.

Monsieur Martinet looked uncomfortable. Even he didn't fancy it. "Let's go round," he said.

"In a barren landscape like this," said Samson Two, "it is difficult to keep your bearings."

"Difficult," said Monsieur Martinet, "is what the best do best. MAX!"

"But Dr. Drax said—" pleaded Samson Two.

"Dr. Drax expects us to use our initiative," snapped Monsieur Martinet. "Initiative is how winners win."

I was going to say, "Yes, and getting lost in deserts is how people die." But they'd already set off, even Samsons One and Two. Monsieur Martinet really did have impressive leadership qualities.

The dune reminded me of my dad. Sometimes if he finished work early in the summer we used to go down to the beach and do dune diving. Have you ever done this? You scramble up a dune, then you just chuck yourself off and run, with the sand giving way beneath you and your stride getting longer and longer until your legs are barely touching the ground so it feels like you're falling but it doesn't matter because the sand is so soft. It's nature's own thrill ride.

Before I even knew I'd decided to do it, I'd joined Max halfway up the dune.

I said to him, "Are you ready for this?"

"What?"

"Dune diving. Come on—you must've done it before. Give me your hand."

Looking a bit nervous, he gave me his hand. I said, "Ready?"

"What for?"

"This."

I jumped.

Gobi Desert sand is even softer than Southport sand. At one point I sank in right to my knees. The next step, half the dune seemed to just disappear underneath me.

As we hit the bottom, the others scattered out of our way like skittles and the two of us lay there staring up at the blue sky and laughing our heads off.

Monsieur Martinet looked down at me and said, "And your point is?"

"It's really, really good. I am sooo going to do that again."

"Mr. Digby," said Monsieur Martinet, "you are a child."

I thought for a second he was on to me, but he was just being rude.

I said, "Anyone else want a go?" and started scrambling up again. When I looked back, Samson Two was following me up, and Hasan, and finally even Florida.

When we were halfway up I said, "We could do it from here. Or we could carry on to the top, look over the other side and see if we can spot the flag. And if we can't, it doesn't matter—we still have a monster dune dive."

Everyone agreed and we all scrambled and crawled and helped each other up. The last few feet were the worst. I flung myself at the top of the dune and ended up flat on my face. Florida used my legs to help drag herself up. Then so did the others. I wriggled up to the top and peeped over. The whole far side of the dune was in shadow. Not a wavy, blurry shadow but a deep, cool pool of shadow, like you could drink from it. And there, fluttering away in the middle of it, was a bright white flag.

And we could all see that if we'd tried to walk around the dune, we'd have spent hours in the heat and maybe never have found the flag at all. Now we'd be there in a few seconds.

"Okay," said Max. "Let's do it."

We all held hands, took a breath and jumped. Bombs of sand exploded around us as we went faster and faster. I went completely over in an involuntary somersault and ended up sliding down the last bit headfirst on my back. I landed more or less at Max's feet. He was holding up the flag and everyone was cheering.

"Did you invent this dune diving?" asked Hasan. "Because you could make a lot of money from it if you copyright it."

"My dad used to do it with me. Don't your dads do it with you?"

"I think he would say it was a distraction," said Samson Two.

"Mine is too busy," said Hasan.

"Mine is too focused," said Max.

I looked at Florida and said, "What about your dad?"

"Of course," she said, glaring at me. "He does it all the time. Don't you?"

I'd forgotten that I was her dad.

"You have an enjoyable dad then," said Hasan. He looked at me like he thought he might be able to buy me.

I just shrugged and took one of the rocket bottles of water out of my backpack and had a sip. Through the plastic, as I was drinking, I could see them all staring at me.

"Did none of you bring water?"

None of them had. I gave them a sip each and said, "I like to come prepared. It's a dad thing."

We struggled back up the dune and then dune-dived

down the other side again, carrying the flag victoriously aloft, like a cohort of avenging Night Elves.

On the way back, the sun was behind us. Our shadows bobbed about in front of us like mad puppets, while our backs felt like they were on fire. Monsieur Martinet wanted to carry the flag, so I put the distress flare in my bag.

Sometimes we'd see some of the footprints we'd made on the way out. But mostly they'd been blown away by the wind. Unfortunately, the other thing we couldn't see was the Possibility Building.

"It must be miles away if we can't see it," groaned Florida. "It's so big. We should be able to see it from Bootle."

Samson Two explained that it was because the sun was shining straight at the horizon. "The light is so strong it seems to dissolve things."

Then Monsieur Martinet shouted, "There it is!" He pointed way over to the left and there it was. It looked much nearer than I had expected. We were all so relieved to see it that we more or less started running. And it took a few minutes for us to realize that Samson One was shouting at us to stop. "Samson Two," he called, "has something he would like to say." We all stopped running, but no one stopped looking at the Possibility Building. "It's about mirages."

Oh. No. I did remember having quite a bit of trouble with mirages in the Blasted Lands.

Samson Two started to explain how mirages worked—which you probably already know.

Florida said, "What has this got to do with anything?"

"Although you can see the building, it isn't really there."

"Of course it's there," snapped Monsieur Martinet. "You're just looking for an excuse to stop walking. Come on, Max. When the going gets tough, the tough get going."

"I believe the wisest course of action," said Samson Two, "would be to wait until nightfall, when the Possibility Building will be easily visible because it is lit up at night."

"He is a genius," said Samson One, "so we should listen to him."

"The Possibility Building," said Monsieur Martinet, "is easily visible now. I know, because I can see it." And he jogged off, with Max following him.

Samson Two called after them, "If the building is really there, why is it due north? The only thing we know for certain is that it is due east."

"How do we know that?" asked Florida.

"Because we followed the shadow of the Possibility Building. The sun rises in the east, so the shadow was pointing west. Now we want to go in the exact opposite direction."

Hasan said, "I want to go with them. It's boring here."

Eddie Xanadu shrugged. "Whatever makes my little boy happy," he said.

Florida said, "I'm bored too. I'll come with you."

They set off.

"How can we stop them?" said Samson One. "They will be exhausted and dehydrated and will probably die."

"Well," I said, "it's their own fault for not listening."

"That's true. But all the same, she is your daughter."

I'd forgotten that. I yelled, "Florida! Come back!"

She glanced round. "Come back, who?" she shouted. I didn't need the instruction book to know she was testing me. If I said "Princess," she'd be so pleased she'd come running back. But it seemed like a better idea to just threaten her. I yelled, "Come back now or else."

"Or else what?"

"This." They'd all forgotten that I had the distress flare. I pulled it out of my bag and held it over my head. "If you don't all come back right now, I'll set this off and the whole trip will be over."

Florida stared at me. They all stared at me. I said, "Okay, come back now. All of you."

They came back. They weren't happy about it, but they came back. Florida was howling. "It's *boiling.* We're never gonna get there by standing still. We're probably going to boil to death. Or die of boredom."

"I'm sure we'll find something to pass the time," I said. "What about sand angels? Like snow angels."

I lay on the ground and moved my arms up and down to make the shape of wings. Then I stood up again. It looked nothing like an angel. It looked like a dip in the sand.

"Or we could write funny things in the sand," I suggested, "in huge letters. Come on, think of something funny."

Florida took the flag and used the flagpole to write one word, "starving," in massive letters.

Until then we'd been too busy being blasted by wind and sand to think about food. All of a sudden we couldn't think of anything else. We put together what food we had.

As emergency supplies for a desert expedition, it wasn't impressive. Florida had a surprising amount of Haribo. Hasan had a supersize bar of chocolate, which had melted into a kind of goo inside the wrapper. We took turns licking the foil. The goo got sandier every time we passed it round.

Samson Two had two raw eggs. "Protein is very good for the brain," he said. No one much fancied them, but when he cracked them open they weren't raw at all. They'd sort of baked in the heat.

Max had a couple of bananas. "Breakfast of champions," said his dad. They'd baked inside their skins.

It didn't take long to eat what we had, and people were

starting to get restless again when Eddie Xanadu said, "In fact, I have something that might be helpful." He unzipped his little bag and took out a thermos flask. Why would anyone need a flask to keep things warm out here? When he unscrewed the lid, a little plume of cool blue mist rose from it. The flask was full of soft, white, chilly ice cream. Everyone sighed and leaned forward. It made you feel cooler just to look at it.

"Of course," said Samson Two, in a kind of dream, "vacuums can be used to keep things cold as well as warm." And he started explaining why.

"They also," smiled Eddie, "keep things creamy. And vanilla-ish." He took a teaspoon, dug it into the ice cream and handed the first spoonful to Florida, saying, "Ladies first."

Florida closed her eyes as the ice cream slid down her throat.

I said, "Florida, say thank you."

"No need to thank me," said Eddie Xanadu, "but I would be grateful for your vote this evening. If not, no second helpings!"

All the dads immediately started shouting, "That's not fair," and, "That's bribery!"

"Not bribery." Mr. Xanadu smiled. "Initiative, which, as you say, Monsieur Martinet, is what winners use. Of course, if you don't want your children to have any . . ."

Now all the kids started yelling it wasn't fair. Eddie Xanadu clasped the thermos to his chest and pretended to look disappointed. "No one wants any?"

"We ALL want some," growled Florida, "and we'll all vote for you."

"It's so nice to be appreciated," smiled Eddie.

They carried on pushing and shoving until every last scrap had gone. It was just about to be my turn when Samson Two shouted, "There it is!"

And there it was, straight ahead of us—and not way over to the left at all—the Possibility Building, like a great big lipstick in the corner of the sky.

After a few minutes it suddenly went dark. There was no sunset. It was more like God had put the light out. And then the building seemed brighter and nearer and we all started walking more and more quickly. Then the light around the building seemed to change from yellow to a kind of strange bluey silver and we saw why—rising up behind the building, so that we could only see the edges at first, was the biggest moon that any of us had ever seen. It was so big and fat and round, like a yellow tunnel, you felt that if you kept walking, you would eventually walk through the horizon and into the moon.

For a while we all stood still and watched it, as though

we thought that once it had finished washing the world in a weird blue light it might do some other trick.

As the moon rose higher, the stars came out. The stars of the Gobi Desert are not the same as the stars of Bootle. For one thing, there were a lot more of them—millions of them—in clusters and knots, and they shone as bright as headlights. We mostly walked with our heads in the air—trying to spot shooting stars and pick out constellations all the way back to Infinity Park.

While Dinah Drax was collecting the votes, Samson One came over to me and said, "If it had not been for you, we would still be walking out there. When no one would listen to my son, you made them listen. Without you, perhaps we would be dead."

"Well, I don't know about that—" But it was true. I had completed my mission. If we were in-game now, all my reward points would be flooding in to me. My health would be going up. And my wealth. And I'd probably have a few more skills too. It was different in-life. My reward was going to be votes.

Of course they weren't going to vote for Eddie Xanadu just because he gave them ice cream. They were going to vote for me. Because I saved their lives. All of them.

"Gentlemen," said Dr. Drax, "the votes from today's little

excursion are as follows. . . .

"Mr. Xanadu, all four votes. Thank you."

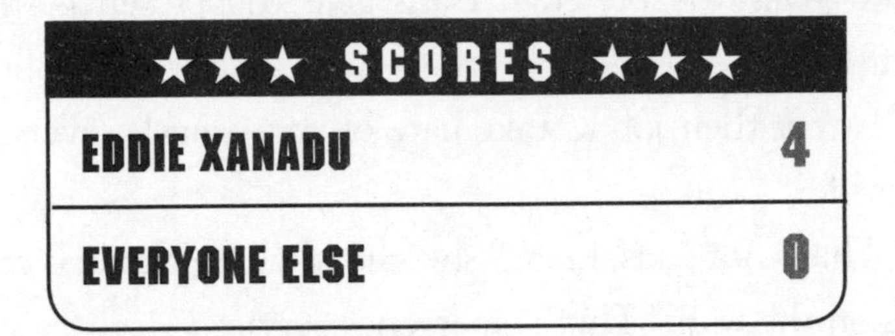

★★★ SCORES ★★★	
EDDIE XANADU	4
EVERYONE ELSE	0

Even though I'd saved their lives, even though I'd found the flag and given them water, even though they *said* I was a good dad, they still voted for the ice-cream man. Even my own daughter!

> *If your teen does something that hurts you, your priority is to find out why. Perhaps he or she didn't mean to hurt you. Say to your teen, "You hurt me when you did that. Let's talk about why you did it. Let me get in touch with how you feel inside."*
>
> *from* Talk to Your Teen

Later on I tried this technique on Florida. I said, "What made you vote for Eddie Xanadu and not me?"

She said, "He gave me ice cream and you didn't."

"That's the only reason?"

"That's what dads are for, isn't it? Why do you think Father Christmas is called *Father* Christmas? He's a father, so he gives you presents. Dads give you presents—that's their job."

"Isn't it their job to take care of you—maybe even save your life?"

"That's not dads, Liam," she said, flicking through channels on the wall. "That's emergency services."

I Can't Work My Trousers

On my fake program for the South Lakeland Outdoor Activity Center, it says, "Day Three—Nature Walk and Tree Recognition."

On our actual third day in Infinity Park what we really did was: Space Suits, an Introduction.

I remember walking into the Possibility Building, just popping with excitement. I was talking to Florida about my favorite game-and-movie space suits. "Have you ever played Orbiter IV? The space suits in that are just cosmic. . . ."

"Liam," said Florida, "you are very undadly."

"What?"

"Dads do not play Orbiter IV. Dads do not say things are 'cosmic.' And most of all, dads do not get excited about clothes. When you go clothes shopping, dads don't say, 'Great.' They say, 'Do we have to?' Then, when you get to the shop, the dads all sit together outside the changing rooms, looking bored."

I said, "Florida, a space suit is not clothes. A space suit is *equipment*. It'll probably come with an instruction manual and everything. It's a gadget. All dads love gadgets. This is a dadly occasion, not a girly shopping date."

The moment she saw us, Dr. Drax said, "Oh, Florida, thank goodness you're here. Let's you and I make this session into our own little girly shopping date."

Then they talked for about ten years about extraterrestrial color coordination. Vehicle Escape Suits are always bright orange, because orange is the most visible color at sea. But Florida was worried that orange would clash with her unfeasibly red hair and Dr. Drax could see her point.

"I totally understand. You'd look like a massive satsuma. On the other hand, a massive satsuma would be very, very visible."

While this was going on, all the dads were sitting together feeling bored. Florida was right.

Eddie Xanadu smiled at me. He said, "I was thinking—in a way you saved our lives yesterday. You found the flag. You made us listen to Samson Two. You are a good guy, I think. It's a shame I got all the votes. I hope you have no hard feelings?"

I said, "No, of course there's no hard feelings," but I think he could tell that I meant, Next time, we'll stake you out, cover you with your own ice cream and leave you to the man-eating ants.

"Good man. Maybe you'll join me in a little drink." He pulled out another flask—this one was silver and had his initials written on it in diamonds. "This makes the time go faster," he said. "Don't let anyone else see." He passed it to me behind his newspaper.

I wasn't sure why no one was supposed to see. Maybe it was because everyone would want some and he only had a little bit. He said, "It's made from plums. In my own village. Where I grew up. In the autumn time, we have a great fiesta."

"Thanks. I don't think I've ever had plum juice. What's it like? Ribena or something?"

I took a swig. It didn't taste like Ribena. It tasted more sort of like being shot through the throat with a laser. All the muscles in my body concertinaed up and then tromboned out. Then my eyes opened so wide that I thought they were going to fall out.

"Good stuff, eh?" smiled Mr. Xanadu. "More?"

I tried to say "No, thanks. Not now. Not ever," but all that came out was a wheezy little croak, which together with the huge-eyes thing made me feel that I had very possibly been turned into a frog. I managed to gasp the words "Thank you."

Then Dr. Drax gave us our escape suits and said it was time to try them on. I tried to say okay, ready when you are. Unfortunately my jaw wouldn't open and close properly. Well, it opened, but it wouldn't close up again.

Vehicle Escape Suits aren't really space suits. They're more sort of wearable lifeboats that you only wear during takeoff and landing, just in case something goes wrong. Something seemed to be going wrong with mine because everyone else got into theirs quite easily but I wasn't able to work the trousers. I could see the hole where your leg went in, but every time I lifted my leg up, the hole disappeared. I put my hand up and said, "Dear Dr. Drax . . ." I don't know why I called her that. "Dear Dr. Drax, my suit doesn't work."

"When you say it doesn't work . . . ?"

"My trousers are malfunctioning."

"In what way?"

"In a very, very bad way that makes my head have a funny hurt."

"Mr. Digby," she said quite sternly, "have you been drinking?"

"Yes! Yes, I have been drinking! You're right. Would that affect them, do you think? It doesn't affect my other trousers. If you can't put them on after drinking, then that is a design flaw. In my humble opinion."

Eddie Xanadu said he would help me, which he did by holding open the leg of the trousers so I could get my foot inside. I said, "Mr. Eddie Xanadu, you are my shining armor knight. My shining armor knight, that's what you are."

"If we may continue . . . ," snarled Dr. Drax. "The most innovative and useful feature of these suits is this . . ." She pressed a button on her suit and—slowly at first, but then faster—the suit started to swell up. "The suit is inflatable, as you see . . ."—hers was still growing—"and if you pull your own cords, like so, yours will do the same." Everyone pulled like so. Everyone started to swell up. "They will be at full capacity during takeoff and reentry so that instead of being strapped in, you'll all be packed in snugly together, like huge peas in a flying pod."

My suit was still growing. I suddenly noticed everyone else standing in a row, very still and serious but also unusually orange, like a police lineup of criminal tangerines. And suddenly I knew I had to bump Eddie Xanadu very hard with my massive orange belly. So I did. Dr. Drax shouted at me. "Mr. Digby," she shouted, "grow up!" And for some reason this made me feel really, really sad. My mom never told me to grow up. She actually told me to *stop* growing up.

Mr. Xanadu had tried to stay standing up but I'd really bumped him quite hard. He fell into Monsieur Martinet. Monsieur Martinet fell into Samson One, Samson One crashed into all the children and the next thing I knew everyone—even Dr. Drax—was rolling round the floor like huge orange marbles, all yelling and shouting for help. I did try and help Dr. Drax back onto her feet, but she batted me away.

"Deflate your suits!" she yelled. "Do not try to stand up until you have deflated your suits!"

I thought suit deflation was going to be hilarious. I thought we'd pull the plugs on our suits and then go jetting off around the room like balloons. Sadly it didn't work like this. We didn't jet anywhere; we just sort of wilted.

I can see now that I probably should not have tried to make up for the disappointment by running round and round with my arms out making raspberry noises. I can see now that this was hardly dadly behavior, but at the time I sort of expected other people to join in.

Monsieur Martinet snarled, "You're acting like a child again, Mr. Digby."

I snapped back at him, "Well, someone has to. And it's not going to be these so-called children, is it? Look at them. They all look so *cross*. They're not like kids at all. They're like unusually small teachers."

I knew I wasn't making much sense and for some reason that depressed me even more, so I curled up on the floor and went to sleep.

On reflection, that wasn't one of my better days. But I think I was right about the children. Hasan fretting all the time about money. Max always making sure he was first. Florida too, going on about color coordination and stuff. They weren't proper kids. They were like trainee grown-ups.

They're like kids now though. Now that they're lost in space.

When I woke up I was in bed. This was so unexpected that at first I thought I'd been abducted by aliens. Especially as someone seemed to be trying to drill a hole in the top of my skull. Then I thought I was probably in Bootle and that the whole Infinity Park thing had been a dream. So I shouted, "Dad!"—which really hurt my head—and then Florida came in and said, "I have had the best afternoon!"

"What happened? Why is this bed so *small?*"

Florida ignored me. "Everyone was really lovely to me. They felt sorry for me because they thought I had a horrible, useless alcoholic dad. You do realize you got totally drunk, don't you?"

"Drunk? How?"

"Mr. Xanadu's flask. He said he tried to stop you. . . ."

"He didn't."

"Everyone was so nice to me. It was like having three dads. And I've got the best space suit. It's blue. Like the Blue Power Ranger. I look great in it. It's definitely my color."

I groaned. "Do we have to?"

"What?"

"Have a girly conversation about clothes and colors and stuff."

"Space suits aren't clothes, idiot. Space suits are equipment."

"Oh really?"

And Florida told me all this amazing stuff about the history of space-suit design. I'll say that again. Florida Kirby told me about the history of space-suit design. This was actually more unexpected than being abducted by aliens.

She explained that because space is such a hostile environment, the space suit has to be like a kind of mini Earth, like a wearable planet, giving you oxygen and keeping you at a constant temperature when space is freezing or when it's boiling, shielding you from radiation and keeping you at the right pressure. On Earth the air is pressing down on you all the time, and that's sort of what keeps you in one piece. But there's no pressure in space so you have to make your own. Usually that means you have to wear a big suit, like a bag, full of gas, so you're walking round inside a big bubble of air pressure. It works but it's clumsy and people are always looking for something better—like a really tight suit that puts pressure on you just by being too tight. Like a wetsuit but tighter even than that. The trouble is, anything that tight would be really painful and difficult to put on. But Dr. Drax had come up with a solution—literally. Liquid space suits. Space suits that you spray on. Apparently they're like thick paint, quite sticky at first but then they cool into something hard but supple—like rubber. Florida showed me a photo on her Draxphone. She really did look like a Power Ranger. Apparently, before they spray the paint on, they put these wires all over, with tiny motors in them, which you activate by twitching. Stick-on muscles, in other words, so that you can jump like five feet on Earth—and maybe twenty feet in space. There are also pipes and stuff so that you can wee and so on without taking the suit off—because to take the suit off you need a solvent spray and about an hour. Much too long if you're really desperate.

Like I said, all this stuff was amazing. But the really amazing thing was that it was Florida who was telling me. Florida Kirby was talking about air pressure and gravity and stuff. I said, "Florida, how do you know all this?"

"That's what we've been talking about all day."

"Yeah, but how did it go in?"

"I'm not thick, you know. The other dads were amazed that I didn't know about pressure and gravity already. And even more amazed when they found out I couldn't swim."

"I didn't know you couldn't swim."

"Exactly. That's what Monsieur Martinet said. He said you were a drunk who took no interest in me. We had to swim in this special pool to show that we could use the suits in weightless conditions. They were really shocked that I couldn't swim. They said that one of the main functions of being a dad was teaching your kid to swim. They taught me to swim—Samson One explained about buoyancy and stuff and Monsieur Martinet threw me in the deep end. Mr. Xanadu said he'd buy me my own pool if I swam a length. They all said it was a tragedy that a unique child like me should have such a thoughtless father like you."

"Can I just remind you that I'm not your real dad? I'm just someone who used to sit behind you in Year Six. The person who didn't bother to teach you to swim, that's your *real dad*, not me."

I knew right then that I'd said the wrong thing because she went quiet. Not quiet like Sunday morning. Quiet like Varimathras, Dreadlord of the Plaguelands, uploading a terrible new weapon.

I said, "Florida . . ."

She said, "Don't speak to me."

"I just . . ."

"Don't *speak* to me."

"I didn't mean . . ."

"*Don't* speak to me."

"I've never even met . . ."

"Don't speak to *me*!"

"But . . ."

"Don't you ever ever ever talk about my dad again. Okay? Not now. Not ever. Never. My dad, let me tell you, is amazing. My dad travels all over the world. That's why he named us after faraway places. He buys me presents. He calls me Princess. He does *not* forget my birthday!"

She stormed out, slammed my door, then slammed her own door.

Talk to Your Teen has one thing to say about what to do when your teenage daughter slams a door—leave it slammed. Don't go near her. Let her calm down. The book made it sound like if you tried to open the door you'd dematerialize or something.

I just sat by myself and watched another repeat of *Celebrity Séance*—the one where Dracula comes on and complains about being misunderstood. "All I ever did was impale people on wooden stakes, which wasn't that unusual at the time. My negative image was all media spin, et cetera."

Suddenly Florida's door banged open again and she yelled

at me, "Excuse me. I'm upset. You're supposed to come and cheer me up."

"Errrm, no. By slamming doors, you're marking off some personal space for yourself and the best thing is for me to respect that need."

"What are you on about?"

"It's in this book." I showed her the bit about banging doors in *Talk to Your Teen*.

She said, "That'd work if you had a TV in your room. But I was getting bored in there."

"You could always read a book."

She stared at me. I said, "Joking."

Then she stared some more. "You really think I'm thick, don't you?" Her bottom lip was starting to go. "Maybe I am thick."

I was really scared that she was going to cry. I said, "Florida, don't cry. I've read the bits about when teens cry and it says you have to hug them. Please don't make me hug you."

"Well, reassure me then."

I said, "You're not thick at all. Who said that? You know loads of stuff—just not the right stuff, that's all."

"What d'you mean?"

"Well, you're really good at remembering things. You know all those celebrities' names, and who they're going out with and everything. You're very good at storing and retrieving information. It's just that it's not very useful information."

Florida was starting to look a bit better. "It was good today when they were all sitting round explaining to me about buoyancy and pressure and stuff. I was like—so *that's* why we don't just fall into millions of pieces. I never even thought about it before. Did you know all that already?"

"Some of it. I'm in Gifted and Talented, you know."

"Maybe you could teach me stuff. You are supposedly my dad after all, and dads teach their kids stuff, don't they?"

"They're supposed to, yeah."

"Only my dad's been too busy. Because he's so important. But you're not busy or important. You could help me get to know stuff. And I could show you how to be a better dad. Because this book is rubbish."

"Okay."

Florida looked thoughtful for a bit and was surprisingly quiet. Then she said, "You know when your in-box is full on your mobile and you delete old messages? Can you do that with your brain, do you think?"

"Mmmm . . . not sure. Why?"

"Cos my brain is full of un-useful information and I was thinking of deleting all of it and filling it up with useful information instead. What d'you think? Or maybe new good stuff could just force out the old stuff. Like if I learned about gravity, I'd forget about Jennifer Aniston's alleged struggle with depression."

"You wouldn't need to delete anything. Your brain's got loads more storage capacity than a mobile phone. You can put new information in with no need to take old information out."

Florida smiled. She looked different. Happier than I'd seen her look in ages. "So I can be clever and stupid at the same time? Cool!"

Oh. Strangely, someone voted for me that day. Everyone got one vote. I assumed that mine was from Florida, but she said it wasn't. It must've been someone whose idea of a good dad was someone who couldn't work his own trousers.

★★★ SCORES ★★★	
EDDIE XANADU	5
M. MARTINET	1
SAMSON ONE	1
ME	1

The Vomit Comet

When the alarm woke me the next morning, it still felt like there was someone trying to drill into the top of my head. Florida explained that it was a hangover. You get them from drinking too much alcohol. She said the best cure was a big fried breakfast. "But we're not supposed to eat this morning. We're going on one of the rides."

"My thrill-ride days are over."

"Liam, you've got a hangover. It's no big deal, not if you're a grown-up. Grown-ups get them all the time. Just drink some coffee and when you see the others, make a joke about it."

"Okay. And Florida . . . thanks."

Even though it wasn't finished—there were still diggers and workmen everywhere—you could see Infinity Park was definitely going to be the World's Greatest Thrill Park. There were gardens and lakes and lots of half-built rides in the shape of rockets. The entrance was a huge arch in the shape of two rockets crossing each other. Outside the gates was just endless beige desert and mountains. Inside, everything was bright colors and trees and waterfalls.

As we drove around in the little Caterpillar minibus thing, Dr. Drax acted as our tour guide. "In Infinity Park," she said, "some of the rides are not ordinary fairground rides. They can be demanding and dangerous—that's why you have to train to go on them. And that's why you have to do exactly as you are told at all times. Sorry. The insurers make us say that. Any questions?"

Hasan put his hand up. "Can we have a proper breakfast now?" he said.

"No. Any more questions?"

"What about a packet of crisps?"

"No. Nothing."

"Why?"

"Come and see."

She took us to a kind of meadow with rockets instead of trees, like a rocket orchard. At the far end was a plane.

"Looks like an ordinary plane," said Dr. Drax. "Not too different from the kind of plane that takes you on holiday. Except it doesn't have any windows. And it's not taking you on holiday. It's taking you on a parabola. Quite a few parabolas, as it happens. Does anyone know why?"

Samson Two's hand shot up. "Zero gravity."

"Oh, Samson Two, aren't you clever?"

"In fact," said his dad, "he's officially a genius—"

"Today," Dr. Drax went on, ignoring him, "you are all going to have a little taste of how it feels to be weightless. Excited?"

We were.

"Any more questions?"

"Can we have just one packet of crisps between us?" said Hasan.

"Hasan," Dr. Drax said, "this plane is officially called the Draxcom Zero Star. But the people who've been testing it have been calling it something a bit more informative—the Vomit Comet."

"Oh."

"Because most people who ride on it throw up."

"Ah."

"So no crisps."

"No."

The outside of the Vomit Comet might look like an ordinary plane, but the inside certainly doesn't. There's only one seat—a long bench thing with lap belts. The walls are completely covered with giant white cushions. There's nothing else in there but a big empty space. "You could think of it," said Dr. Drax, "as a kind of giant soft-play area flying through the air. There. That's a nice, cuddly thought, isn't it? Sick bags are under the seats. Good luck."

While we were strapping ourselves in, Florida whispered, "What does she mean, weightless? We're going to lose weight?"

"Sort of. . . ." I started trying to explain about gravity but then the engines started up. And we were taking off. I don't mean like a normal takeoff. The Comet seemed to be heading straight up into the air for ages. We had to hold on to the bench so we wouldn't slip off. And the ringing in our ears was so loud we thought we'd never hear anything else again. I felt like my head was going to explode. It was not enjoyable. Everyone was trying not to think about what was going to happen, which wasn't easy because Samson Two was trying to impress Florida by describing the whole thing—how we were going to climb to some amazing height and then dive faster than we would fall if we were shot down.

Max wailed, "Dad, tell him to stop talking!"

Monsieur Martinet looked at him sternly and said, "Max, there is no point trying to hide from fear. Fear will find you. You have to look fear in the eye, say hello and keep walking by. Remember, Fear is the Enemy of Courage."

"Yes," shouted Samson Two, "you must understand that you feel more fear than normal partly because of the unusual amount of gravity acting on your pituitary gland. It's being squeezed and is therefore pumping out more adrenaline than usual. You should just enjoy it."

Max stuttered. "But . . ."

"Max," snapped his dad, "I insist that you ENJOY IT!"

"LET ME OFF!" wailed Hasan.

"You know," said Eddie Xanadu, "there are rides like this in America. Only they cost four thousand dollars each time. Don't think of it as a scary experience. Think of it as a bargain."

Florida was gripping my arm. But I didn't feel too bad. The higher we climbed, and the more my ears hurt, the more I thought I'd had this feeling before. Then I remembered where. I turned to Florida and said, "The log flume."

"What?"

"It's just a big log flume. You remember, how it takes you ages to chug up to the top of the ride and then you roll over the top and . . ."

"Oh yeah," said Florida. And she relaxed her grip a bit.

"It's a twenty-thousand-foot log flume. The only difference is, you won't get wet at the end."

She grinned at me. Thinking of it as a log flume made it feel different. Suddenly the feeling in our ears wasn't just horrible air pressure—it was excitement filling our heads like a balloon. A voice on the loudspeaker said, "We are now approaching the crest of the curve. Please unfasten your safety belts and prepare for a zero-g interlude."

"This is it!" said Florida and she let go of me completely, put her arms in the air and screamed, just like on the log flume. Unlike Monsieur Martinet, who grabbed my other arm even tighter.

"I remind you," said the loudspeaker voice, "that your sick bags are under your seats."

Monsieur Martinet still didn't let go. He hadn't undone his seat belt and he didn't go for his sick bag. He was just sitting there, breathing deeply with his eyes shut, gripping my arm. I tried to prise his fingers off me.

Then it happened.

I stood up, pulling myself out of Monsieur Martinet's grip, and tried to walk. The first step was longer than I expected. The second was a lot longer and on the third I just took off.

For a whole second I was flying headfirst down the plane like Superman. But my feet kept going upward so I ended up doing the first double somersault I'd ever done in my whole life. I said, "Whoo hoo!" or something. And when I came up I was facing Florida. She jabbed me and shouted, "Tag!" and the jab sent me spinning back the other way. When I came up this time, I was facing Samson Two. Before I even thought about it I tagged him. He looked completely surprised and confused. Like no one had ever tagged him before. I tried to swim off—that's what it felt like, swimming in the air—but suddenly it was all over. One of my feet touched the floor and before I knew it everyone was standing on the floor again. Except Monsieur Martinet, who was still strapped into his seat.

Florida was whining. "Why's it called the Vomit Comet? No one was sick." She sounded like she thought I should do something about it.

Then that voice came on the loudspeaker again and said, "That was the first parabola. Please prepare for the second."

"There's more!" said Monsieur Martinet, and grabbed my hand again.

So it all happened again. The plane climbed, our ears hurt, Hasan said he wanted to get off and then we all started floating again.

Someone thumped me on the back and sent me somersaulting down the plane. When my head came up, I could see Samson Two grinning at me and shouting, "Tag to you too!" He put his thumb up.

Suddenly a voice yelled, "Stop!" and there was Monsieur Martinet, still in his lap belt, but a bit floaty, like a balloon on a string. "The pilot has lost control!" he bawled. "This is an emergency! We need help! We need—" but instead of words a ball of puke slipped out of his mouth and drifted off down the plane like a tiny green planet.

"Look!" yelled Florida, pointing at it as if it was the most exciting thing in the world ever. She got herself in front of it, opened her sick bag and let the vomit planet drift inside. "Back. Of. The. Net!" she yelled.

When we were all back on the floor again, Florida showed me the sick bag and said proudly, "Caught it."

"I know."

"Want to see?"

"Not really."

She also tried to show it to Dr. Drax when she landed. I did try to discourage this. "Florida," I said, "I'm sure Dr. Drax doesn't want to see that."

"Oh, but I do, I do." Dr. Drax smiled. "I was watching on the monitors and I have to say, Florida, the coordination and agility you showed when you caught Monsieur Martinet's little accident was very impressive. I think you have the makings of an excellent taikonaut."

Florida glowed a kind of radioactive pink and looked round to make sure that everyone was listening. No one was. Everyone was staring at the plane. A little girl with her hair tied back with a ribbon and her hands held stiffly at her sides was trotting down the steps of the plane and onto the tarmac. We were all thinking the same things—how did she get on there? Where was she when we were all floating around? She looked about Florida's age, but the way she stood next to Dr. Drax reminded me of Mrs. Sass standing on the stage at assembly—still and straight, waiting for us all to be quiet.

"Ah," said Dr. Drax, "I'd like you all to meet my daughter, Shenjian. She was piloting your plane today."

Eddie Xanadu said, "Surely you're teasing again."

"Not at all. This," said Dr. Drax, "is what Infinity Park is all about. Giving children the chance to show what they can do. Although Shenjian is only thirteen—"

"Thirteen?!" shrieked Monsieur Martinet.

"—she is an excellent pilot."

Everyone gasped.

Shenjian said, "Infinity Park believes in young people. This is why I started training as a jet pilot when I was nine years old. Astronauts of the future must be young so that mankind will be able to make longer journeys. I am the future."

You could see that Dr. Drax was enjoying how amazed we all were. She said, "Any questions?"

Florida said, "That's a lovely coverall. I like the detail on the pockets. Will we be getting ones like that?"

"Possibly."

"They look very astronauty. I'd love one."

"Any questions that are *not* about clothing?" snapped Dr. Drax.

"This is very inspiring," said Samson One. "Samson Two can do things that many adults cannot do. And when he was only thirteen Alexander the Great was already a great leader. Although of course, even Alexander the Great was not flying jets. Because they hadn't been invented."

After that the grown-ups had to go and see a doctor for finger pricks and blood pressure.

"Mr. Digby," the doctor said when it was my turn, "you have the metabolism of a twelve-year-old. You'll have to tell us your secret." And she winked at me!

Monsieur Martinet was next in line. He said, "I believe he has the brain of a twelve-year-old too. When the pilot lost control of the plane, this man tried to start a game of tag!"

"The pilot lost control of the plane?" said the doctor. "I heard that it all went very smoothly."

"They have to say that," said Monsieur Martinet, "for insurance purposes."

Florida was waiting for me when I came out of the doctor's room, which is unusual because she usually just gravitates toward the nearest television. She was still radioactive pink and worryingly smiley. She said, "How did that happen?"

"What?"

"How did we just start floating around like that?"

She was being so nice. My game skills told me to suspect a trap but I couldn't help enjoying her treating me with respect like this. I started to explain about the Earth having gravity which keeps you on the ground and how if you go far away from Earth you have less gravity so you float.

"Yeah, but what *is* the gravity? I mean, how does it work?"

"Well, all objects exert gravity. And big objects—like planets—they have enough gravity to pull things toward them. Like the Earth attracts the moon and the moon attracts the sea."

"What are you talking about, the moon attracts the sea?"

I tried to explain tides and stuff to her, but the more I tried to explain how it worked, the more I realized I didn't really know.

"Liam," she said, "you don't really know, do you?"

"No."

"We'll go on Wikipedia tonight and find out."

"You do know that *Celebrity Dental Check* is on TV tonight?"

"We can skip that. It's the one with Tom Cruise, where they find out that his teeth are completely false. Like you couldn't already tell."

I was sure I was going to get all the votes. After all, I was the only grown-up who actually liked being weightless. I got one vote. In fact, everyone got one vote again. I said to Florida, "What is the point of the voting? Who is ever going to vote against their own dad? Except when someone pays them not to, in ice cream."

"I voted against you," said Florida.

"What?! Again? Why? You said you were going to help me."

"I voted for Monsieur Martinet."

"You . . . what? Why? He was scared! He passed out on the runway! He *threw up*."

"I know. Wasn't that great?"

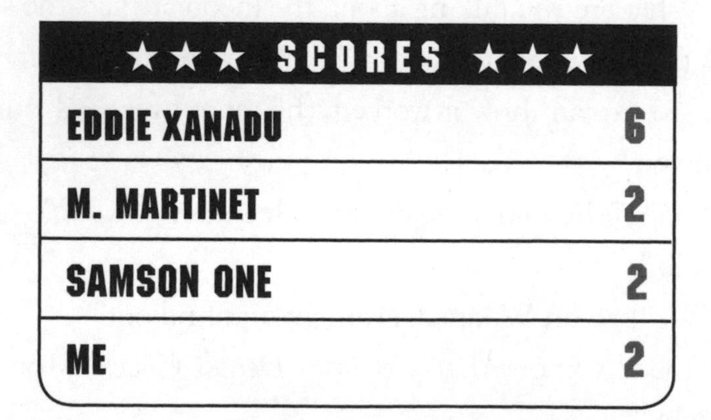

★★★ SCORES ★★★	
EDDIE XANADU	6
M. MARTINET	2
SAMSON ONE	2
ME	2

Astrogossip

That evening Florida really did spend lots of time on Wikipedia trying to find out more about gravity and space travel.

She looked on all the right pages, but she has a brain that turns everything into daytime TV. So she accidentally invented a whole new field of knowledge—astrogossip. She'd say stuff like, "Valentina Tereshkova—she was the first woman in space—on *Vostok* 6—and guess what? She married another spaceman. . . ."

"Astronaut."

"Cosmonaut. And they had a space baby! How cute is that?! A cosmonautette."

I sort of preferred it when she was talking about Britney's ghost dog.

Gravity Is Not a Trivial Monster

In the middle of Infinity Park is this dome, the Infinity Dome. The outside is all mirrors, so that when you walk toward it, you see yourself walking toward you. The entrance is just a narrow door, with the mirrors bending inward. As you get closer, you just melt into your own reflection, like entering a portal to another dimension or something. Inside it's completely cosmic. The dome is where all the best rides are. These are not rides like you've seen before. Their names are all to do with the history of space exploration: the Giant Leap, Lake of Fear, Sea of Storms. The biggest one—the Vortex—looks like a kitchen blender from the Land of Giants. When we arrived that morning, it was whirling round so fast on its spindle it looked like it might come loose and take off. There was an old man named Mr. Bean in charge of it. I mean, he looked old but he also looked young—his eyes were bright and shiny and he walked like he was weightless. He gave us this big hello when we arrived, pressed some buttons and the Vortex slowed right down.

"You'll never guess what's in here." Dr. Drax smiled.

No one had any idea of what could possibly be inside a twenty-foot blender. Dr. Drax nodded at Mr. Bean. He winked at us, then pressed some more buttons. The door opened, a ramp appeared and down the ramp came . . . Shenjian.

Everyone gasped. "You were in there?!" said Florida. "How could you be in there? If they spun me round like that, I'd turn to soup."

Shenjian bowed and then stood up straight to show she wasn't soup.

"The Vortex," said Dr. Drax, "is really just a big washing machine. When you're ready, we're going to pop you inside and spin you round until you feel like old knickers. How does that sound?"

"Uncomfortable," said Florida.

"It certainly will be. At first. But soon you will be able to cope with it, just like Shenjian. Look, she's not even dizzy."

Shenjian bowed again, to show that she was not only not soup, she was not even dizzy.

"Yesterday we had great fun finding out what it was like to experience less gravity than usual. Today you're going to get a taste of what it's like to experience a lot *more* gravity than usual. That's what happens when we spin you in our centrifuge. Excited?"

Somehow being whirled in a massive washing machine didn't seem as appealing as floating around inside a big airplane.

Florida was still trying to get her mind round the whole gravity thing. "If less gravity makes you float in the air," she said, "won't extra gravity make us sink into the ground?"

Samson Two giggled. Max tittered. Samson One rolled his eyes. Monsieur Martinet snorted.

A few days ago I might've laughed too, but now I felt different. I said, "No, Florida, you won't sink through the floor but you'll feel heavy."

"You are going to experience 10 g," said Dr. Drax. "That's ten times your normal gravity."

That's more than twice as much gravity as you get on the Cosmic. I tried to imagine a version of the Cosmic that was twice as big as the one in Enchantment Land. The man who runs the Cosmic had said that lots of people passed out at 5 g. We were going to hit twice that. This really was going to be a scary ride.

Mr. Bean opened the steel doors wide. Inside was a big metal arm with a little seat on each end. If Orgrim Doomhammer, Orc Lord of Durotar, had made a seesaw, that's what it would look like.

"So," said Dr. Drax, "you'll weigh ten times more than you usually do."

Florida put her hand up and said, "Are you saying we're going to put on weight!?"

They all giggled again.

Florida didn't react. She knew they were going to laugh at her and she still asked the question. Because she wanted to know.

I said, "You will put on weight, but you'll lose it again the moment you return to normal gravity." And then I said, "Okay, Princess?"

She beamed at me. "Okay, Daddy."

Dr. Drax went on. "I know 10 g sounds like absolutely heaps of gravity, but the body can take more than that. David Purley, the racing driver, once experienced 180 g and lived to tell the tale. If he can do it, so can you."

Samson One said, "That seems like a lot of gravity in a car. How did he do that?"

"He drove straight into a brick wall with his throttle wide open. He was doing 107 miles an hour. Now then. Who's first?"

"Are you sure he survived?"

"Yes, he did. Or did he? I'm not sure. Anyway, rockets are much safer than cars."

Samson Two said, "Are you sure rockets are safer than cars?"

"Course they are," said Florida. "They don't have brick walls in space, do they?"

Monsieur Martinet wanted Max to go in first because "that's what winning is all about." But Max wouldn't budge. And when his dad tried to shove him in, he just kept shouting, "No! I don't want to!"

Monsieur Martinet was hissing at him, "You're embarrassing me."

Eddie Xanadu tried to bribe Hasan to get in. Hasan wasn't moving either. His dad was snarling, "You're making me look like a fool."

Samson One tried to explain to Samson Two that gravity was just a natural force and nothing to be afraid of. That wasn't working either. Even though his dad was growling, "Think of your reputation."

I said to Florida, "We should go on first. Show them what a good team we are."

"I'm not going in there."

"Did you ever go on the Cosmic?"

"No. I was too short, remember?"

"Pepsi Max?"

"Queue was too long."

"Traumatizer?"

"Too scary."

"Well, I've been on big rides—and this thing here, it's just a big ride. Do you want to know what the worst bit of a big ride is?"

"What?"

"The queue. The waiting. The anticipation. Watching everyone else screaming and turning green. That's way, way, way the worst thing. It's tons better to go first. And if we go first—all these others, all the people who were laughing at you before, they'll have to stand here, watching us and getting more and more scared."

She liked the sound of that.

We strolled past Monsieur Martinet while he was poking Max in the chest, and Eddie Xanadu, who was waving a wad of money at Hasan, and Samson One, who was drawing a diagram to prove to Samson Two that gravity wasn't scary. We walked past all of them right up to the machine.

"Florida Digby"—Dr. Drax smiled—"you certainly seem to have the Right Stuff to be a taikonaut."

Mr. Bean came into the Vortex with us and showed us how to strap ourselves into the seats—one at each end of the evil seesaw. My seat was—obviously—too small. I had to tuck my legs up really tight to get into the harness. Now that we were in there, I could see that Florida was starting to get nervous. I said, "Mr. Bean, has anyone ever died on this?"

"On this old thing? No, sir. Not a one." He taped some wire things to the ends of our fingers.

"Please don't say 'But there's always a first time.'"

"Well now, I'm going to make sure that you're not the first. I'm going to monitor all your heartbeats and whatnot. You start to malfunction, I'll stop the whole thing."

For a while nothing happened. It was just really, really quiet. Florida said, "I'm really, really scared now."

"But just think: if we're really, really scared, *they* must be really, really, *really* scared. And in a few minutes we won't be scared at all. You'll be all right, Princess."

"Actually, you can stop calling me Princess now. It sounds weird when you say it. Thanks all the same."

There was a deafening THUNK. We both screamed. Our chairs jumped sideways, then stopped dead.

Phew! I thought. It's broken.

Then it started.

If you've ever been on the Cosmic, you'll know what 4 g is like—you feel a bit sick and scared, but if you spread your arms out and pretend you're flying, you feel better. As you blast into the air you can think, *This is bad but this is as bad as it gets. It gets easier any second. . . .*

But the Vortex was different. On the Vortex, 4 *g* was only the beginning.

A voice came over the loudspeaker, telling us we were now at 5 *g*. You can't spread your arms out at 5 *g*. You can't move them at all. It feels like the air has turned to concrete and you're stuck in it. It's hard to breathe, but you think, *We must be near the end now. We must slow down now.* But we didn't slow down. We went faster.

The voice said we were at 6 *g*. Now my eyeballs felt like little shriveled raisins. I couldn't see anything except a muddy blur. But still we didn't stop. We went faster.

At 8 *g* you feel flat, two-dimensional, like Itchy and Scratchy run over by a steamroller. I thought I was dead. I was even starting to enjoy being dead when I heard the voice again, saying we were now at 10 *g*. The sentence didn't come and go like an ordinary sentence. It seemed to stay in my ears, steady, like the noise of a humming top. Then my chest exploded. But the air was so thick that all the bits of me couldn't fly away. They just stayed there. In the same shape but not connected anymore.

Then we slowed down.

And that was just like Itchy and Scratchy too. When the steamroller's gone and someone comes along with a foot pump and pumps them back up to their normal shape. Amazing. For a minute I didn't say anything because I thought if I opened my mouth I might deflate again. I looked over at Florida and she said something like, "Ha ha ha ha ha ha ha ha ha ha ha!!!!!! Whoooooo!"

And I said, "Cock-a-doodle-doo!" which is not something I usually say.

The door opened. I was so proud of us that I tried to stroll out and swagger past the others. Unfortunately I seemed to have lost my swagger-control skills and ended up swaggering sideways.

"Sit down, Florida; sit down, Mr. Digby. Take a rest. You've done very well."

I think she probably meant us to sit down *on* something, but as soon as she said it I let my legs go and so did Florida. We just sort of plonked ourselves down on the floor.

Monsieur Martinet was still hissing at Max.

Eddie Xanadu was pleading with Dr. Drax to let Hasan be excused. "Dear little Hasan really doesn't want to do it."

"I'm afraid dear little Hasan will have to do it. Unless he doesn't want to go to space."

I thought, Some people just have NO CONTROL over their children. And everyone went quiet and looked at me.

Apparently I'd thought this out loud. Very loud.

"So," snarled Monsieur Martinet, "you think you can do better?"

"I think I already did." I shrugged and pointed at Florida. She gave him a cheeky little wave.

I should've left it at that. But now that he'd said it, I *did* think I could do better. Samson Two was now squealing, "*I'm not going. I'm not going. I'm not going. I'm not going.*" And to think they'd laughed at Florida! It would serve his dad right if I could get his son to go in there when he couldn't.

I decided to Engage. "Hey, Samson Two, what's the biggest ride you've ever been on?"

He looked blank.

"Have you been on an inverted roller coaster?"

"No."

"An ordinary roller coaster?"

"No."

"Inverted bungee?"

"I was on a seesaw once."

"A seesaw?"

"Not a real seesaw—it was really a large model used for demonstrating the action of vectors around a fulcrum. But while my father wasn't looking I sat on it. Sorry, Father."

"So there was no one on the other end of the seesaw?"

"No. But I solved that problem easily by propelling myself

upward with my legs repeatedly, in effect making myself into a vector."

"And that's the only ride you've ever been on? A one-ended seesaw?"

"It was fun."

No wonder he was scared. Imagine going on something like the Vortex if you've never even been on a proper seesaw. I tried to explain to him about rides, about how in a few months' time the dome would be full of people paying money, queuing up, desperately wanting to go on the Vortex. For fun.

"But why won't they be scared?"

"They will be scared. They'll be terrified. But they want to be terrified. It's a nice feeling. A tingly feeling. And they'll be with their friends, and their friends will be teasing them and daring them. You know, we're very lucky. We've beaten the queues."

He looked over at the Vortex and said, "Okay, I'll go." I grinned at Samson One, thinking, That'll teach you to laugh at us. Then Samson Two said, "As long as you come with me."

"What?"

"You say it's fun. You must want to do it again."

"Well, I wouldn't . . . it wouldn't be fair to your dad if I took his turn."

"I don't mind," said Samson One a bit too quickly.

"Well, maybe Dr. Drax wouldn't agree."

"It's hard to fault the child's logic, Mr. Digby," said Dr. Drax, "and once you're rested there's no reason why you shouldn't go into the Vortex again."

It wasn't so bad the second time. The only trouble was I was just thinking to myself, This seat is tiny. I'm really uncomfortable and I can't move, when we came to the bit where Time stands still. So that big, depressing thought just sat there in the front of my brain for ages and ages, blotting everything out and making it all seem worse. So if you ever have to endure a period of prolonged weightiness, my tip is that you try and have a happy thought.

When we'd finished it took Samson Two a moment to get his breath. Then he said, "Is it over?"

"Yes. What did you think?"

"It was very . . . informative."

"Informative?"

"Yes. Gravity's not a bit like it looks in the diagrams."

When we came out, even though it felt like we'd been in there for years, nothing had changed—Hasan was still telling his dad that he wouldn't go in there, and Monsieur Martinet was still poking Max in the chest and calling him a loser. Max was taking no notice. Until he saw me. Then he said, "I'll go in."

"Good boy, Max," said Monsieur Martinet, glancing at Mr. Xanadu. You could see that when he said "good boy," he really meant "Better than your boy."

"As long as I go in with him," said Max, pointing at me.

When I climbed into the Vortex for the third time I concentrated on happy thoughts of all the great stuff I'd done since deciding to be a grown-up—walking in the Gobi Desert and driving a car and flying in a plane when I should've been in Waterloo High playground. Max leaned forward in his chair and said, "I voted for you last time."

"*You* did?!" I wondered who had voted for me. I never thought for a minute it was him.

"I vote for you this time too. I vote for you because I want you to come with us. Not my father. I want you to come because you are a loser."

"A what?"

"A loser."

"I'm not a loser. I'm Gifted and Talented."

"When you were running down the sand dune, that made me laugh," he said. "And when you were rolling on the floor in the space suit. Remember?"

"Not the details."

"When you do stupid things—"

"They weren't that stupid. I just—"

"Will you do something stupid today? Please?"

"I'll give it my best shot."

"Thanks for that."

Then THUNK.

We were off again. Only this time when I got to the Forever bit, instead of thinking about flying and walking in the desert, the word "loser" stuck in the front of my brain and stayed there.

When we came out Hasan was still saying he wouldn't go in. Dr. Drax said, "If the child needs more time to prepare himself mentally, perhaps this would be a good opportunity for the other dads to take their turn. Samson One and Monsieur Martinet can ride together, and then Mr. Xanadu can go on with Hasan."

They looked a bit unsure, but what could they say? They took their turn and this time I got to watch from the outside. To start with, the washing machine chugged round at something like the speed of a light woollens wash. Then it went up a gear to something like colorfast cottons, and after that worryingly fast—like a spin dryer, and then it suddenly started to slow down again. I said, "What happened? Has something gone wrong?"

"No," said Dr. Drax, "that's the complete cycle. They've been in there just as long as you were."

"But I was in loads longer than that."

"They were in just the same time as you were—namely six minutes, including one minute at 10 g."

"One minute?!"

"Why?" said Dr. Drax, examining her fingernails. "Did it feel longer than that?"

It felt like a whole chapter of my life—say, about as long as I'd been at primary school.

When the dads got out of the Vortex, Florida was excited by the possibility that they might be sick. But they weren't.

When they were done, Hasan looked at me and said, "Everyone else went on with you. I want to go on with you."

"I'm a bit tired."

"That's so unfair. Everyone else got to go with you. Why shouldn't I?"

Dr. Drax said she really thought I had made my contribution already today.

Hasan said, "Daddy, tell him he has to go on with me."

"I'm afraid your daddy can't tell him that," said Dr. Drax, "because it isn't true."

Eddie Xanadu sidled up to me and said, "How much to make it worth your while, Digby? A watch? A car perhaps?"

"A car? No, thanks."

"I don't think you'll be able to bribe Mr. Digby, Mr. Xanadu," said Dr. Drax.

Then Hasan said to me, very quietly, "Come on with me and I'll vote for you."

And I realized that though Mr. Xanadu couldn't bribe me, his son really could.

Knowing that the lifetime at 10 *g* was only a minute made the fourth time easier. I was just starting to get my happy thoughts ready when Hasan said, "There was a war in my country."

"Oh yeah?"

"Soldiers came to our village. They wanted to take away all the children. But my father paid the most important soldier some money so that he wouldn't take me away."

You could hear the engine warming up outside. Hasan started to talk more quickly. "That's why he loves money. Because it can help."

"Well, fair enough."

"And the reason he always wants more money. I watched all my friends being taken away, all the children from my school. I watched our house burning down."

He told me this. And then the engine started. And in my head I saw Glenarm Close, Bootle, all in flames, and

Mom and Dad and Florida all being taken away by soldiers. That's what I was thinking when I got to the Forever bit.

I was still thinking about it when the ride was over. But Hasan was grinning. He said, "That was *fantastic.* I could do that again." I suppose anything is fantastic compared to having your house burned down and your mates led away. He bounced out of the machine.

"Don't forget to vote," I called after him.

★★★ SCORES ★★★	
ME	6
EDDIE XANADU	6
M. MARTINET	2
SAMSON ONE	2

Everyone had voted for me.

Last Chance to Vote

The Penultima is called the Penultima because it's the next best thing to being in space. On the outside it looks like any other simulator but bigger. When you walk inside, though, you are standing in the biggest, best flight simulator ever built. It's a full-size replica of the *Infinite Possibility* command module—five seats, multifunctional displays, even a PlayStation 3 for the boring bits of the voyage. You can tell they think it's going to be a major attraction because it's right in the middle of the Infinity Dome and the queuing lane is about a mile long. How much did Florida love strolling past the "Queue takes 45 minutes from here" sign! "It's like this for a lot of celebrities," she said. "I read that they opened Chessington World of Adventures early once, especially for Brad Pitt and all his kids."

We spent the morning on the Penultima, learning how to guide a rocket through reentry. "Of course," said Dr. Drax, "on the big day, all that will be taken care of by those clever people over at DraxControl. But we want you to learn how to do it, just in case."

There was a monitor shaped like a window. You could see the Earth, with clouds and seas rolling across its big curvy face. As the Earth got bigger you could just make out the glowing border of space and the atmosphere.

Mr. Bean showed us what to do. "Think of that glow," he said, "as the flap of an envelope. Just slip under the flap and you're on your way home. It's as simple as that. It's all about the angle. Max, you're first."

Max stepped up to the control panel and tried to steer us in. There was a kind of arrow on the screen to show you the angle. What you had to do was keep the front of the module lined up with it. Max would probably have been all right if his dad hadn't been standing behind him saying, "Steady, Max, steady," over and over. The more he said it, the less steady Max got, until suddenly, just as the glow was getting clearer, everything changed. The Earth spun around—continents and oceans whirled into each other. Then the entire planet completely vanished and everything was black.

"Now, you see what's happened here," said Dr. Drax, "is that Max didn't get the angle just right—"

"I told you to watch the angle," snarled his dad. "Why didn't you watch the angle?"

"—and as a result," said Dr. Drax, "the rocket has bounced off Earth's atmosphere, a bit like when you skim a stone off the surface of the sea. My father, by the way, was rather wonderful at skimming stones. His record was twenty bounces."

Through the "window" there was nothing but blackness punctuated by stars as we rocketed farther and farther into space. Florida said, "Can't we reverse?"

"Not now. We're drifting out of control."

"But we'll stop in the end? Everything stops in the end."

"Not in space. In space you just drift on forever."

"Yes," agreed Samson Two. "It's Newton's first law of motion, I'm afraid. Unless an external force is applied, a body will remain at rest or will continue to move at a constant velocity. Forever."

"So," said Florida, "if we bounce off the atmosphere on the day, what do we do?"

"Hold on tight and enjoy the ride." Dr. Drax smiled. "But don't worry—it won't happen. Show them, Shenjian."

Dr. Drax reset the simulator and Shenjian took the controls. As we got nearer to the Earth, she read out all the changes in gravity from the monitors.

"She's doing that just so that we down on the ground can hear that she's awake," said Mr. Bean. "A lot of people pass out during reentry. Also, it's hard to move your hands.

You've just got used to weighing nothing when—*ping*—you weigh a ton."

The blue seas and the white clouds looked so friendly and familiar, and then they were gone. The screen was filled with a blazing golden fire.

"We're dead again!" yelled Samson Two. Shenjian didn't even blink. "Or perhaps the machine is malfunctioning?"

Shenjian just kept saying the numbers.

Mr. Bean said, "We're not dead and it's not a malfunction. That glow is just us slamming into the atmosphere. We're moving so fast all the little atoms on the outside of the rocket are shedding their electrons. It's a pretty thing, isn't it? Of course, you'll have no time to appreciate it when it's actually happening."

Shenjian shouted, "Gravity five and rising."

Samson Two said, "That means she's back inside the atmosphere."

"On your way home, Skylark," smiled Mr. Bean. "Mother Earth is holding your hand. Just don't let her drop you."

And the golden glow flew away like wrapping paper, leaving the blue Earth looking as new as a present.

All of the children had a go at the reentry procedure. It made my fingers itch just watching them. Because the fact is, the

Penultima—the world's most accurate rocket simulator—is just a big version of Orbiter IV—a game at which I am a consistent high scorer. Even the control-panel layout is the same. Reentry is a task you have to master to get past Level Seven in Orbiter IV.

I was twitching to play, but the other dads didn't seem to be paying any attention at all. Monsieur Martinet said that watching the others reminded him of driving lessons, and the next thing they were all going on about cars. Monsieur Martinet said he drove a Mercedes and Mr. Xanadu said he had some Mercedes too "for midweek, you know." Samson One said he preferred Land Rovers because of living in the desert, and they all started on about four-wheel drive. They talked about cars as though they were playing Top Trumps. Sometimes they made me feel like I was the only grown-up there.

"What about you, Mr. Digby? What do you drive?"

"A car."

"But what kind?"

"A blue one. . . ." I was trying to concentrate on the Penultima. "I don't know much about cars."

"But you drive for a living. Surely you have to know about cars?"

I'd forgotten about being a taxi driver. I said, "It's more about knowing your way round town really. The car's just . . . tools of the trade really." I remembered what Dad had said about taxi driving. "Taxi driving is about people, not about cars. You have to be a bit of a psychologist, a bit of a tour guide, a little bit of everything. I don't really have time to be interested in cars . . . I even delivered a baby once."

I think probably the baby thing was going a bit far—though Dad did sort of deliver a baby once. Everyone stared at me, like they were going to ask me to prove it by delivering another baby right now. Luckily Mr. Bean told Monsieur Martinet it was his turn at the controls.

Monsieur Martinet slipped inside the golden envelope just as neatly as Shenjian had. He crossed his arms and said, "Child's play." Then the screen went black and the simulator said, "Permanent Fatal Errors. Uh-oh, you are dead."

"I don't think so," he snapped.

"Not quite yet," said Dr. Drax with a smile, "but in a very few seconds. You forgot to open your parachutes."

Next up was Samson One, who bounced off the atmosphere and toward the sun. It didn't bother him. He seemed to quite like the idea of accelerating until you turned into a beam of light.

Mr. Xanadu seemed more interested in trying to buy the Penultima than he was in steering it. "Such a great machine.

If you sell it to me, I will add fighting monsters and lightly clad female aliens to the simulation. It would be popular and profitable."

"The simulator is part of our training program," said Dr. Drax. "Fighting monsters is not one of our training objectives."

"But with a little work," said Eddie Xanadu, "this could make your fortune."

"I already have a fortune, but thank you for your suggestion."

As she said this, he hit Earth's atmosphere hard in a kind of interplanetary belly flop and burst into flames. "Marvelous graphics!" he said. "Please take a picture of me at the controls like a true taikonaut." He gave me his phone and got the children to pose and smile with him.

Then it was my turn. I don't want to brag about this, but I have completed Orbiter IV Level Fifty, when you have to do reentry while being chased by a giant squid. So it really wasn't hard. Even so, Dr. Drax was impressed. "Would you mind doing it again just to make sure that wasn't beginner's luck?"

This time they tried to trap me. An unexpected meteor shower went by during the final approach. Luckily this is a standard Orbiter IV trap. You just have to remember that meteors have a gravitational pull of their own and correct your coordinates accordingly. If you don't, you get pulled off course. I was into the golden envelope for a second time.

Afterward, during the voting, Samson Two asked me why I was so good at the Penultima. I said, "Don't tell anyone, but I've got a PlayStation game just like this."

"You play PlayStation?" said Samson Two.

"A bit. I prefer massively multiplayer online games like World of Warcraft."

"Those are unusual activities for a dad," said Samson Two.

"But it turns out they're good activities for a taikonaut."

Samson Two smiled, nodded his head and then went off and started whispering to the others. Then all the children went off to vote. I knew I was going to win. I was the only one who would be able to save them in an emergency. I did the math in my head. Eddie and me were both on six. That meant if I got three, I'd definitely won. But I could still win even if I only got two, as long as the other two votes didn't both go to Eddie.

When Dr. Drax came back in with the results, my heart was popping with excitement. "The children have decided," she said, "who is the best daddy in the world. And who is going to be the best daddy in space. He got four votes today. . . ."

Four votes. It had to be me. I was going to space!

"He is Mr. Eddie Xanadu!"

Eddie got ten points altogether. I came second with six.

I did ask the children about it. "I just like having my photo taken," shrugged Florida.

"But I can work the machine."

"Yes," said Samson Two, "you were the best at handling the rocket. But that means you are also the best at PlayStation. We don't want a grown-up who is good at PlayStation. When people are good at PlayStation, they don't get killed for hours and hours and you have to sit and watch them, waiting for your go. We don't want some console hog. We want someone with no PlayStation skills."

That's the scary thing about children. They will vote to go into space with someone who is dangerously useless if it means they get a longer go on the PlayStation.

I Am Half a World Away

Dr. Drax wanted all the children to move into a special crew house now, opposite the Possibility Building, so that they could get used to living together and to Mr. Xanadu being their "responsible adult."

Florida got a blue "crew member" suitcase. I watched her running about the bungalow getting her clothes and toothbrush and stuff together and I had this really strange feeling in my throat. At first I thought maybe it was some sort of gravity-related problem, but that was daft. We don't have gravity problems on Earth.

Then it hit me.

Worry.

I was worried about Florida Kirby.

After all, she was going into space.

Without me.

Who was going to look after her? I'd just got used to being

her dad and now she was going away.

I said, "Are you sure you're going to be all right, Florida?"

She said, "All right? I'm going to be famous. Like Buzz Lightyear—"

"Buzz Aldrin."

"—or Laika the dog. She was just some mongrel, but after she became the first animal in orbit she was the most famous dog ever. They made Laika chocolate bars, Laika soft toys. She was on postage stamps. They wrote songs about her. And she was just a stray. They don't even know what breed she was really. There she was, wandering the streets of Moscow with two other dogs. The next thing Laika was really famous. And she was only a dog," she said. "Imagine what it's going to be like for us—the first kids in space. What's up with you?"

She must have seen me flinch. I was thinking, Laika *died* in space. What if . . . ?

"Oh, I know," said Florida. "You're jealous because you're not going."

"Who says so?"

"I say so."

"Me? Jealous of you!?"

"As if you're not."

"As if I am." I was acting like a kid. I know that. It seemed easier than doing the dadly thing and telling her I was worried about her. I kept thinking of her sitting on top of a two-hundred-foot firework blasting into orbit. What kind of dad lets his child do that?

Then I had to take her to the crew quarters. That was the worst bit—watching her walk away. She didn't even look back and wave. She was chatting happily to Samson Two. They looked so tiny as they passed the Possibility Building.

I thought of all the times in my life that I had wanted Florida Digby to go away, and here I was wishing she'd turn around and come running back.

It was a strange, unhappy thing being on my own in the bungalow that night. I sat up on the couch watching TV all night. Sometimes I'd nod off in the middle of *Celebrity Séance* and wake up in the middle of *Celebrity Dental Check*, then nod off again and wake up in a different episode of *Celebrity Séance*. When the first bit of daylight crept into the room I thought, Right, now I'm allowed to have a bacon sandwich. I couldn't find actual bacon but I did find some thin pink meat-stuff with "Explodes the Tongue" written on the packet. The explodes thing must've been some kind of warning though, because the minute I put it on the grill it burst into flames and all the smoke alarms went off. Standing there in the kitchen with greasy smoke billowing round me and sirens wailing in my ears reminded me of home.

Which is probably when I rang my mom.

The phone rang for a surprisingly long time before she answered.

"Hello?" She sounded like she'd never heard a phone ring before.

"Mom, it's me, Liam."

"Liam? Are you okay?"

"Yeah, I'm great."

"What are you doing?"

I looked at the timetable for day six at the South Lakeland Outdoor Activity Center and I said, "Pond dipping. We went pond dipping and I caught . . ."—I lost my place—"um, a water boatman. That's a big beetle which has seen a steep decline in its population recently."

"What else?"

"Climbed on the new fifty-foot climbing wall and came down on the ever-popular but very safe aerial runway."

"That's great, Liam, and you weren't frightened? It hasn't given you nightmares?"

"No."

"And you're eating okay?"

"Yeah. Food is plain but wholesome, cooked here on the

premises. We're expected to help clean up afterward. It's a team-building activity."

"And you're sure you're okay?"

"Yeah. Great."

"Really, really sure?"

"Why d'you keep asking if I'm okay?"

"Because you've just rung me up."

"I can ring you up, can't I?"

"Liam, it's the middle of the night."

"Oh."

"Oh" was the best I could come up with. I put the phone down.

I'd completely forgotten about the time difference. I think that was when it hit me that I was half a world away.

Compared to where Florida was going, I was just around the corner.

I felt really lonely that night. I think it must be the only time I've been in a house on my own at night. And now look—I felt bad on my own in a house. Now I'm on my own in the universe.

If Anything Goes Wrong . . .

Next morning all the dads—including Eddie Xanadu—had to meet Dr. Drax in a bar inside the Dome. Magnificent Desolation, the bar was called. "I just have one or two more things for you all to sign," said Dr. Drax, passing round some forms and also a drinks menu. "These are mostly legal waiver forms, saying that you understand the dangers of space flight and you're giving your children permission to go, so that if anything does go wrong—not that anything will—you as the parents will be responsible."

I didn't really want to think about things going wrong so I just concentrated on the drinks menu. I couldn't believe it when the others all asked for coffees and teas. There were so many drinks to choose from. I spotted something called the Cosmic Quencher, which I had to order because "cosmic" is my favorite word.

Dr. Drax was explaining that the whole mission was

Top Secret. "If anything goes wrong—not that it will—we will not admit that the mission ever took place. Because of course if anything does go wrong—which it won't—the bad publicity would close Infinity Park. I'm sure none of you wants that to happen."

I said, "When you say if anything goes wrong, well, what could go wrong exactly?"

"Oh, you know how people make a fuss," said Dr. Drax. "If someone breaks a toe or gets a headache, then people will say it's too dangerous. This is our first attempt. If it doesn't go according to plan, we're not going to say it'll be better next time; we're going to deny it ever happened." Then she smiled and said, "You're a man of the world, Mr. Digby. You understand."

I do understand now, by the way. I understand because something did go wrong—so wrong that Dr. Drax probably denied that this mission ever took place. Which means no one down there is trying to help us. No one is calling International Rescue, or the X-Men, or whatever. No one is scrambling to a superfast rocket to come and save us. Because no one knows we're here. No one knew where we were going. And no one knows we didn't get there.

The Cosmic Quencher turned out to be a bucket of Coke with two big dollops of ice cream bobbing about in it, decorated with little silver stars and a bunch of sparklers blazing away in the top. I imagined all the others were thinking, I wish I'd ordered one of those instead of my boring coffee. I suppose they might have been thinking, That is not a dadly drink. But I didn't care about that anymore.

While we were signing the forms, Eddie Xanadu kept going on about how pleased he was that he had won. "I never thought I would go into space. Or rather I did. As a child, of course I watched the Apollo missions on television. I thought I was living in the space age. I thought we would *all* be going to space. I was disappointed. Until now. I remember my father took me to see some samples of moon rock when it first came back. . . ." The other dads remembered queuing up to look at moon rock too. "And that was also disappointing because it was gray. I expected it to be glowing, like the moon in the sky."

All the other dads laughed. Then Samson One said, "Surely even a child knows that the moon has no innate luminescence, that it only shines because it reflects the sun."

Mr. Xanadu shrugged. "We all make mistakes." And the other two nodded as if it didn't really matter. But it did really matter! How could they let their kids go into space with someone who didn't know that the moon had no innate luminescence? Before you go on a quest you make sure you've got all you need: skills, equipment, money, health, magic elixir. . . . What did he have? Nothing. He was just a big, grinning, empty-headed troll. And we were entrusting our kids to him. I tried to say nothing. I know politeness is dadly and yelling is not. I did try not to Engage. I stood and listened quietly while he said, "The important thing is that the children have decided I am the best dad. And I will *be* the best dad, not just to Hasan, but to all of your children, I reassure you."

Everyone clapped except me. Before I knew what I was doing I was on my feet, saying, "Well, it doesn't reassure me.

"How can we let our children go into space with a man who doesn't even know that the moon has no innate luminescence? How can we let our children go into space at all? Space isn't safe. What kind of dad lets their child go into space?"

They all muttered stuff about it being a great opportunity, the opportunity of a lifetime. And Samson One said, "After all, Dr. Drax's own daughter is going."

"Well," said Dr. Drax, collecting in the forms, "not this time."

"Not this time?"

"No. In fact, Shenjian is running a temperature so I've decided to keep her back. It may be just a cold, but it could be measles."

Shenjian can't go to space today because she's got a

temperature. She made it sound like she was going to skip PE.

I said, "But Shenjian is the professional taikonaut."

"Really, Mr. Digby, there is so little for the crew to do. All the hard work will be done by those brain-boxes at DraxControl. You know, in 1969 the Americans landed a man safely on the moon with less technology than you've got in your Draxphone. The equipment they had then was sticks and stones compared to what I've built here."

"So it's completely safe?"

"We have a policy here at Draxcom. It's called Massive Overprovision. That means, for instance, that there's ten times as much oxygen on board than they could possibly need. Twice as much fuel. Even the layer of Kevlar on the module is three times thicker than necessary, so it's three times as bulletproof."

"Bulletproof? Why would it need to be bulletproof? Does the man in the moon have a shotgun or something?"

"Oh, you know, in case of meteors."

I hadn't even thought about meteors. I said, "You know, thinking about it, I don't want my daughter to go into space. It's too dangerous. Yes, it will be a great opportunity, but she can have great opportunities here on Earth where she won't be impacted by meteors."

"It does you great credit, Mr. Digby, that you are so concerned about your daughter." She was already walking away while she said this, taking Eddie Xanadu with her.

I stood up and almost shouted, "I'm withdrawing my permission."

"But legally speaking," she said, waving one of the forms in the air, "you've already given your permission. Have a nice day."

And she closed the door behind her.

You Don't Get Extra Lives in Space

I could barely even finish my Cosmic Quencher. I went over to the Possibility Building to look at the rocket. I thought it would make me feel better to see it, looking so solid with its extra oxygen tanks and its extra bulletproofing. Mr. Bean was there, looking up at it too. I said, "Mr. Bean, has anyone ever died on this?"

"On this particular rocket? No. This is what you call an expendable launch vehicle. You're only supposed to use it once. A bit like one of those throwaway razors. You can't really know that an expendable will work until it's already up there—and by then it's too late."

The thought that they were going to space in a throw-away razor wasn't particularly reassuring. It got worse. "People do get killed on rockets," he went on. "Gus Grissom, he died when *Apollo 1* caught fire on the launchpad, along with Ed White and Roger Chaffee."

"Oh. Right."

"But that was a long time ago. This is a different kind of rocket. If you're looking for something more recent . . ."

"Well, I'm not looking exactly. I was just asking."

"The crew of the *Columbia* shuttle—they all died on reentry. There were seven of them. The crew of the shuttle *Challenger* all died on takeoff. Seven of them too, all really young."

I did say then, "Thanks, I think you've answered my question." But there was no stopping him.

"And then there was *Soyuz 1*, when the parachute didn't open. Vladimir Komarov. That was awful. He knew he had no chance. Everyone could hear him talking to his wife on the radio, talking about the kids and, oh—"

"Honestly," I said, "that's enough information. Thank you." I began to walk away.

Mr. Bean called after me, "Going into space isn't like one of those video games. If you die, you don't get any extra lives."

That's when I decided I was going to go and drag Florida out of the crew quarters and take her home to safety. We could walk home to Bootle if we had to.

Obviously it would be better to go in a plane, so as I strode across the rocket tramway lines and the bridge over the fire pit I was rehearsing this speech I was going to make to Dr. Drax, about how it would be better for everyone if she gave us the airfare. But as I got nearer I could hear shouting and saw a Draxcom personnel vehicle screeching up to the crew quarters. Dr. Drax was yelling, and Mr. Xanadu was yelling back at her and throwing his bags into the back of the car.

As the car drove away, Dr. Drax turned to go back into the house. Then she saw me and she looked really surprised.

"Mr. Digby!" she said. "How did you know? I suppose you guessed. I should've guessed myself, of course."

I didn't know what she was on about. "Mr. Xanadu," she said, "has totally betrayed me."

It turned out that when Mr. Xanadu was cheerily taking all those photographs of the Penultima he wasn't really interested in happy smiling faces. He was taking photos of the flight simulator and the control panels. He'd sent the photographs to a toy company in Shanghai, asking them to build a full-size working replica of it for Hasan.

Sadly for him, Dr. Drax also owned the Shanghai toy company.

"They told me everything. He even went to them with an idea to make dolls out of you all—to sell. He was going to call them the Astrokids. Can you imagine? Where do these people get their ideas? At least no harm has been done. Except to Mr. Xanadu, of course. He will no longer be the responsible adult accompanying the children into space. That honor will go to the person who came second in the competition. Namely you, Mr. Digby."

"Oh."

"Give yourself a moment for the news to sink in."

Somehow it seemed to take more than a moment. Somehow my brain wouldn't work.

She said, "Mr. Digby?"

"You mean, I could go to space?"

I looked over my shoulder. It was nearly a mile away but there was nothing between me and the Possibility Building. It still filled most of the sky. I was standing in its shadow.

"You do know, of course, what those letters say?" Dr. Drax pointed at the huge black Chinese letters up the side.

"No."

"They are the slogan of Infinity Park. They say, 'The World is My Thrill Ride.'"

"But that's—"

"That's what you said to me on the phone that day. That's why I specially selected you. It seemed to sum up everything I was trying to say. You know, Mr. Digby, I always knew you'd be the one who'd go to space in the end. You remind me very much of my own father. You have a similar quality.

A sort of childlike quality."

I could hear the other children talking and laughing behind her. I could feel the cool shadow of the rocket on my back. Was it different if I was going too? Was it all right to send my daughter to space if I was going with her? All I had to do was say "Thank you," and I would be riding the rocket.

I took a deep breath and I said, "Dr. Drax, I know you think I'm a responsible adult but I'm not. I'm just a boy. An unusually tall and hairy boy, but a boy."

I felt better straightaway. Like gravity had somehow decreased and I was sort of floating. There. It was all over. No more pretending. No more responsibility. I didn't care what she said to me now.

Dr. Drax just smiled. She touched my hand. She said, "That's exactly what I mean about you. You have the right quality. You feel like a child inside. So did Einstein, all his life. He said he never stopped thinking like a child. That's why he made these great discoveries—"

"No. I don't mean I feel like a child. I mean I'm really not grown up."

"Perfect. Exactly. Anyone who feels they're all grown up is no use to this project. It's the people who feel they've got nothing left to learn—"

"Exactly. I haven't finished school. I've hardly started."

"I feel just the same way. The universe is so huge. We've barely glimpsed it. Give me someone who knows he knows nothing over someone who thinks he knows everything, any day."

"But—"

"By the way, take good care of Hasan, won't you? It's a hard time for him. He'll be disappointed that his father isn't coming. And upset, because obviously I'm suing Mr. Xanadu for every penny he's got."

"Oh. Really?"

"Yes. I'm determined to put him in jail for what he did."

"Right. Was there anything else you wanted to say?" I thought it probably wasn't the best moment to tell her I'd been lying to her for weeks or that I'd tricked her into putting me (aged twelve and a bit) in charge of her rocket (cost $1 billion).

"In fact," she said, "can you sign this while you're here? It's a release form, giving me permission to use your wonderful phrase—'The world is my thrill ride'—on all our publicity. Just there. Thank you. And it only remains for me to say, enjoy the ride."

The Real Thing

As we went into the crew quarters, Dr. Drax said it was nice that I was going to see my daughter on this particular day. I wasn't sure what she meant. When I got inside the house the place was full of balloons and piles of crumpled-up gift wrapping.

Florida shouted, "Hi, Daddy! Where's my present?"

I said, "What present?"

"Oh, stop teasing," said Florida, grinning at everyone. "He always remembers my birthday really."

It was Florida's birthday!? How was I supposed to know that? How did everyone else know?

"Dr. Drax told everyone. She knew because it was on the forms. Look what Mr. Xanadu got me. . . ."

It was a doll—like a Barbie—but it wasn't Barbie. It was Florida in her blue Power Rangers space suit. It really looked like her, like she'd been miniaturized by a wicked supermage.

When you squeezed it, it said, "What do you mean, weightless? Am I going to lose weight!?"

"How cool is that?" smiled Florida. I knew right away what it was. It was a prototype of one of his Astrokids dolls.

"What did you get for Florida, Mr. Digby?" said Hasan. "We've been hearing about the time you bought her the pony."

"Oh really?"

"And also about all the great party games you play. Will you show us a card trick?" said Samson Two. "They interest me psychologically."

"Maybe later. Just now I'm going to give Florida her present. In private."

We went into the kitchen. I said, "Why didn't you tell me it was your birthday?"

"You're supposed to know. You are my dad, you know."

"I am *not* your dad. I'm only pretending. Remember?"

"Are you saying you haven't got me a present?"

"I'm going to give you a birthday treat. This is it: I'm going to save your life." I told her everything—all the stuff about this being a secret mission and Shenjian having the "measles."

Florida said, "Ken Mattingly."

"What?"

"Ken Mattingly was supposed to go on *Apollo 13* but he was pulled off at the last minute—just like Shenjian—because of German measles. And after that everything went wrong and they all nearly died. He suffered terrible guilt feelings for the rest of his life—'My *Apollo 13* Guilt Hell.'"

"That's it, exactly. They were in Terrible Danger, and we're in Terrible Danger. We've got to get out of here. You thought it was bad when I nearly drove a Porsche. A Porsche goes 170 miles an hour. Do you have any idea how fast the *Infinite Possibility* goes? We are in trouble."

"You're my dad—get me out of it."

"No. That's just it. I'm not your dad. I can't do card tricks. I didn't get you a pony. And I don't call you my little princess."

"But—"

"Ring your real dad."

"What for?"

"We're in trouble. He can get us out of it. He's a dad. That's what he's for." I was thinking how simple it all was. Florida would ring her dad. He'd probably go nuts. But, from then on, I would no longer be in charge. I wouldn't have to be a grown-up anymore.

Florida said her dad was too busy and I should ring my dad instead. I said, "That wouldn't work. Besides, what can my dad do? He never goes anywhere. Your dad knows about these things. He could be here in minutes. He could—"

"No one can get to China in minutes, Liam. He's not Superman."

"No. But he is your dad. He won't want his little princess blasting off in a rocket to space, will he? Especially when he finds out the only person who knows anything about flying rockets isn't coming and the so-called responsible adult is twelve years old."

I gave her my Draxphone. I told her to call. Now. Before it was too late. She fiddled with the phone for a bit and then she said quietly, "Liam, I haven't got a dad."

I didn't understand. What she'd just said didn't make any sense. "What d'you mean?"

"I mean I haven't got a dad. It's just me and Mom and Orlando and Ibiza."

"But your dad travels the world. That's why he named you after faraway places."

"We never go anywhere. My dad left just after Orlando was born. I don't know where he is. He had a big row with Mom and never came back. Even when he was there, he never did any of the things I said he did. You know—taking pictures, buying ponies, anything like that. He just used to sit watching the holiday channel. That's where he got our names from."

This was unexpected. I said, "Okay. Well, if you did have

a dad . . . if you had a dad now, he would not let you sit on top of two hundred feet of inflammable fuel. He would not let you be sent up into the air at thousands of miles per hour. He would be very, very concerned at the thought of you experiencing 40 g. He would be worried if you went on a big ride. And this is not a ride. The point is, this is not a ride. This is the Real Thing."

Florida looked a bit surprised.

"But, Liam, if I got famous, my dad—wherever he is in the world—he'd see me, wouldn't he? And he'd come back and find me. Or at least he'd know about me, you know? He'd go round telling people he was my dad. He'd be proud of me. That's why I want to be famous. That's why I want to go on the rocket."

I wasn't sure what to say. I think I was probably quiet for a while because in the end she said, "Liam? Have you fallen asleep?"

"No. I'm just thinking." I realized I was all the dad Florida had. It was time to do the right thing, the dadly thing, and give her exactly what she wanted—what we both wanted. There was one of those cardboard party hats on the table—the pointy kind with the tinsel in the top. I found a pair of scissors in the kitchen drawer and started cutting it.

"What're you doing?"

When I finished I held it up for her to see. I'd cut it into a kind of crown. It was a bit rubbish, but it was a crown. "I thought it would be easier to say this if you were actually dressed for the part." I put it on her head and said, "Happy birthday, Princess."

She grinned and said, "You've still got to get me a proper present."

"Okay. I'll tell you what . . . I'll take you to space."

We went back in to the others. They were all standing around, eating cake. I said, "All right, let's get this party going."

They all looked blank. They really didn't know any party games. I made them play grandmother's footsteps, musical statues and this game called fish, where everyone has a fish-shaped piece of paper and you race them by blowing on them. This went on for ages because Samson Two developed a very streamlined fish, which Hasan tried to buy off him. And Max blew so hard he more or less asphyxiated himself. And as it happens, I do know some card tricks—Dad used to teach me them sometimes when I went out with him in the cab, if we were waiting a long time at a taxi stand. The other kids were all amazed and amused. Florida said it was her best birthday party ever.

Quest Orange

In World of Warcraft, the quests are all color-coded. Gray quests involve defeating people with fewer skills than yourself. They're very easy, but you don't gain much experience. Then there are green—a bit harder; yellow—harder still; orange—a lot harder; and red—Certain Death. I decided the best thing was to treat this whole thing as a quest.

Dr. Drax definitely gave us the impression that she was sending us on a gray quest. Maybe a bit green round the edges. But definitely not yellow or orange. And certainly not Certain Death.

For a start, we had loads of backup. She took us to DraxControl so that we could see for ourselves. It's a massive glass office, with huge plants and a little water fountain and dozens of people strolling round in white shirts, talking into headsets, reading their BlackBerries. They certainly looked like they knew what they were doing. "These are the clever people who will be steering your rocket," Dr. Drax said, "so you won't have to do a thing. The *Infinite Possibility* really is just a ride. And DraxControl is like the man in the fairground booth. All you've got to do is be sensible and enjoy the view for a few hours. Oh, and do one simple little thing for me."

And it did seem a very simple little thing. We had to press some color-coded buttons in the right order at the right time. That was it.

Because the *Infinite Possibility* is really a launch vehicle—that's why it's so big. It was carrying something into space. A payload. A completely cosmic payload.

"I'll explain it all to you," said Dr. Drax. "It's a kind of space minibus. I designed it myself. It's called the *Dandelion* because it doesn't have engines—just these big silvery sails that catch the solar wind, just like normal sails catch the normal wind, and blow it across space. A spaceship propelled by sunbeams—as quiet and traceless as a dandelion seed. Hence the name."

She showed us a model. It looked like a high-sided vehicle with lots of windows. Like an ice-cream van. Only with no wheels. And no ice-cream man.

Once it was separated from the *Infinite Possibility*, the people at DraxControl were going to steer the ice-cream van across space, round the back of the moon, and back to Earth by remote control. Then it was going to do a lap of the Earth and head back around the moon. And it was going to keep doing that—one lap of the Earth, one lap of the moon—in a kind of figure eight, forever. It had comfortable seats that turned into beds. Dr. Drax's plan was that as soon as Infinity Park was opened, people would pay to get into a small rocket, dock with the *Dandelion* during its Earth orbit and stay on for one lap of the moon before going back down to Earth.

A sightseeing trip around the moon in an interplanetary ice-cream van.

The *Dandelion* was a kind of massive box just under the living quarters of the *Infinite Possibility.* All we had to do was shoot up into space, float around for a bit, and then, when Dr. Drax said so, press the buttons in the right order—red, orange, green—and that would blow the *Dandelion* off into its own orbit.

Then DraxControl would bring us back home in the command module.

The buttons are designed to set off a series of small explosive charges—red to separate the *Dandelion* from the rocket, orange to blow the covers off the *Dandelion* and green to make its sails pop out.

"We could detonate the charges from the ground," said

Dr. Drax, "but we thought it best to keep it simple."

What could go wrong?

Well, nothing did go wrong, exactly.

Not with the buttons.

Not with the charges.

Not with the *Dandelion*.

The thing that went wrong was us.

Launch Minus 48

Countdown begins forty-eight hours before liftoff.

For the last forty-eight hours we had to stay in the crew quarters and not talk to anyone from outside. It was supposed to be a bonding experience.

Also, all the food in the fridge and the cupboards was replaced with space food. Little packs with straws sticking out of them, a bit like Capri Sun but with meat and veg instead of orange juice. We were supposed to eat space food from now on so that we'd get used to it. The packs had some worrying names—for instance "Saliva Chicken" and "Pork That Makes You Eat Your Own Hand."

Samson Two said it was probably a problem with the translation. "Maybe 'Saliva Chicken' means 'Mouth-Watering Chicken,'" he said. "And perhaps 'Pork That Makes You Eat Your Own Hand' is just Finger-Licking Good.'"

"Maybe," said Florida, "but I think I'll stick to ice cream."

"Me too," said everyone else. So we just sat there sucking on space ice cream (two flavors—"Raspberry Like a Breeze on a Lake," or "Banana Divided") and practicing the color-coded button-pressing on the computers.

During the night there was a clanging sound, like the lid had fallen off the sky or something. Everyone ran into the living room. When I got there they were all huddled together. I was going to get into the huddle too when Samson Two said, "What is it?" And I realized they were all waiting for me to sort it out.

Hasan said, "Is it bears?"

"Bears? Why would it be bears? Wait here and I'll go and look."

I opened the front door, thinking, What if it *is* bears? I couldn't see any. Or smell anything. I could hear a noise though—a slow, monotonous rumble. But I couldn't see anything except the Possibility Building. Then I realized the building had changed shape. I stood and watched for a while before understanding what was going on.

They were moving the rocket.

Very, very slowly it was trundling out on its tracks, out in the desert, about three miles away. It was moving along the rails to the launch site. You could barely see anything happening, but if you looked away and looked back, you could see that a bit more of the rocket had shouldered out of the building. It was like watching the minute hand on a clock. The others all crowded round me and I said, "Come on. Let's get some sleep. It's just the rocket. Nothing to be scared of."

I was thinking, That is so much scarier than bears.

"I want my dad," said Samson Two.

I knew just how he felt.

Next morning there was a pile of presents waiting for us on the dining table—some rubbery pencil-casey-type things called Personal Inflight Packs and five of the latest Draxcom games consoles (they're called Wristations). We'd had a visit from Space Santa. Wristations are quietly cosmic, by the way. They're basically Game Boys that fit on your wrist, but instead of having some squinty little screen, they project the game onto the wall, like in the cinema, so you can have it as big as you like. They all came loaded with Orbiter IV, Stone Age Boneheads and Surfing Eskimos. Except mine, which had Professional Golfer and a test-your-own-cholesterol kit.

There was a note from Dr. Drax explaining that we could pack whatever we wanted in the Personal Inflight Packs (PiPs for short) to take as personal luggage on the trip. We could take anything we liked as long as it fitted in the PiP.

Two minutes later there was a Wristation territorial dispute. Hasan and Max were playing Orbiter IV together on one wall and Samson Two was using another whole wall to play Stone Age Boneheads. So there was nowhere for Florida to play. I started by suggesting that Florida and Samson Two play Boneheads together, using the two-player option, but that suggestion led to immediate offscreen violence. In the end, I told Samson Two to stand nearer the wall to make the projection smaller.

He said, "No."

Everyone stared at me.

It was a test of Dadness.

What was I supposed to do? Beg him? Threaten him? Shove him?

If I couldn't control them here in the living room, what would it be like in orbit?

I moved the couch into the center of the room. I checked that it was lined up with the middle of the wall. Then, without even looking at him, I said, "Samson Two, sit down here," and that's all I said. I did try to make it sound like I expected immediate obedience. Then I held my breath. Samson Two didn't look away from the wall. And he didn't say anything. But he did move forward and around the couch. Then he sat down and carried on playing. His game had shrunk to half size now and there was loads of room for Florida to play.

I said, “Now move right to that end, Samson. And Florida, you sit at this end.” Which they both did.

Hasan and Max weren’t even looking at me now. I’d passed the test.

But what if Samson Two had just carried on saying no?

I decided then and there to pack *Talk to Your Teen* in my PiP. It was really too big. I had to squeeze it in, bit by bit. And as I was nudging the rubber sides over the book’s spine, I noticed all the dad things on it—the two overlapping tea stains, like a figure eight, the phone number written in pen, the gas receipts. It was my dad’s book. My dad. I wished he’d turn up now, like he did when I got into that Porsche. I wished he’d turn up and shout, “Stop!”

Some Kind of Lovely

At launch minus six I was still insanely hoping that Dad would actually turn up. Especially at launch minus six, to be honest. Because at launch minus five they were going to do the spray-on Power Rangers space suit thing.

The thing about the spray-on space suits is that you have to have a bald chest before they put the stuff on you. So, if you're a dad, you have to have your chest waxed. That means they pour warm wax all over you and then rip it off with strips of cloth. When the wax comes off it pulls all your chest hairs out with it.

At launch minus five my dad still hadn't come and I was screaming in pain and looking at a piece of wax covered in curly hairs that had been pulled out by the root.

"There," said Dr. Drax. "The agony of reentry will be nothing after that."

Apparently women do it to their own legs, and they don't

even get to go to space afterward!

After that they sprayed on my space suit—it felt warm and tickly—and I was allowed to go back into the living quarters and wait for it to dry.

When I got there, Mr. Bean was waiting for me. He shook my hand and wished me well. "You take care of yourself now," he said.

I said, "I thought *you* were going to be taking care of us. I thought all *we* had to do was enjoy the view."

He laughed. Then he said, "Since you mentioned the view, there was something I wanted to tell you. You got your PiPs, right?"

"Yes."

"Think hard about what you put in there. It could be your most important piece of safety equipment."

"What? More important than our space suits?"

"Maybe. You see, the thing about space is—"

I said, "—it's full of dead people. You already told me."

"Space is somewhere else. D'you see? It's not just far away. It's a different kind of place. It can get a hold of you."

"Are you saying, 'You'll like it when you get there'?"

He smiled. "My mother used to say that. Did yours?" He looked out of the window. Even though it was daylight, you could still see the moon, pale but huge, like a big balloon. He said, "Did you ever hear of Ed White?

First American to spacewalk. A long time ago now—1965. First American to open a door into space, to dangle from a wire and look down at the Earth and see the whole planet roll by beneath him. He couldn't believe what he was seeing.

"Everything he knew and didn't know. His friends, enemies, places he'd been, places he'd never go, all just sitting there in his field of vision. When it was time to go back inside he couldn't tear himself away. He was like, 'Ah, let me stay a little while, why don't you?' And, 'Isn't that America? Oh no, it's Africa.' And . . . you know. The command pilot—Jim McDivitt—he had to bawl him out somewhat to bring him back to his senses. Do you see what I'm saying?"

I said, "Not really."

Florida had just arrived in her Power Rangers getup. She said we were supposed to keep moving around to check for fissures and flaws.

Mr. Bean went on. "I'm talking about how to stay in one piece. Try to get hold of the things that are important, the good and true things about your life. Up there is some kind of lovely. And maybe you need to have something in your heart, you know, something even more lovely. To help you find your way home. Otherwise maybe you could be beguiled."

"Beguiled?"

"I think that would be the word. I'll say good night."

"Good night, Mr. Bean."

He smiled and said, "Call me Alan."

Just as he was about to go out the door, Florida shouted, "Wait! Alan Bean? *Apollo 12*, 1969? That is cosmic."

It was the first time she'd ever used my word. There probably isn't any other word for being able to touch someone who has walked on Another World.

"Wow!" said Florida. "An Apollo astronaut? That makes you dead famous, doesn't it? I mean, you had ticker-tape parades and went to all these parties, and you were on TV all over the world."

"I wasn't on TV so much, actually. I broke the television camera. When we landed on the moon, I accidentally pointed the camera at the sun and burned it out. Imagine that—we went all the way to the moon and didn't get any holiday footage. So . . . not on TV as much as some! What I remember is being on the moon. I remember every second. Every stone. Every star we saw. Sometimes it feels like I never really came back."

He shrugged. "But I did come back," he said, "and you remember that. Where you're going—it seems far away and dangerous. But you will come back."

Which is more or less exactly what my dad said to me on my first day at Waterloo High.

As soon as Alan had gone I wedged my old phone into

the PiP, because it had pictures of home on it. And Dad's St. Christopher statue. It wouldn't have fitted if it hadn't been a bit broken.

Florida said, "What're you taking that for?"

I said, "Why? What're you taking?"

She said, "Haribo, mostly."

I Want My Daddy

When we left the crew quarters the next day, the dads were all waiting by the transporter, ready to say their last good-byes. Monsieur Martinet, Samson One and Eddie Xanadu with two security guards, one on each side of him. They chatted to their boys, rubbed their hair and punched them in the shoulder. Samson One shouted to me, "Look after my boy, now." I had one last crazy hopeful thought that my dad might show up with the others, but he didn't. At least I had Alan to talk to.

Dr. Drax gave us each a "lighter than air" ice lolly shaped like the *Dandelion*. "A last-minute treat." She smiled. "When Infinity Park opens we're going to sell these all over the world. Aren't they just delicious? Oh, by the way, I have to ask you all to hand in your new Draxphones. Just to protect the secrecy of the mission."

The first thing I did when I got onto the flight deck was shuffle Dad's St. Christopher out of my PiP and wedge it into the instrument panel. The whole rocket was throbbing, so St. Christopher looked as though he was doing some kind of mad dance. The other thing that I found in there was the little credit-card stress tester. As I picked it up it changed from blue to pink and a message appeared. Just one word: "Stressed."

The *Infinite Possibility* was two hundred feet high. At the top you could feel it swaying in the wind. And you could hear the wind rolling in and out of the pipes and engines, sobbing and sighing and generally sounding miserable.

As the Responsible Adult, I had to do all the last-minute checks. All the way through, Samson Two kept spouting space facts. I suppose it was his way of coping. "Do you know," he said, "that exposure to weightlessness makes you grow? Because there's less pressure on your spinal column, it relaxes and that makes you taller."

Just what I need, I thought. A few more inches. I said, "We could have a 'See How I Grow' chart, just to see if it's true. A kind of experiment." I made them all line up so I could mark their heights on the back of the safety door. Just to take their minds off things.

Max suddenly said, "I'm not frightened. When the going gets tough, the tough get going. Also, only the strong survive. And I am strong."

"Yes, but I'm not strong," said Hasan. "Does that mean I

won't survive? Where's my daddy? I want my daddy."

Florida said, "Your dad's probably in jail by now," which didn't help.

The stress tester had changed from pink to scarlet. The message read, "See Doctor Immediately."

I said, "We're all worried about takeoff. Let's stop thinking about it. Let's think about inflating our escape suits. In fact, let's do it."

It hadn't just been the electric Ribena. I was right. It was distractingly funny. The kids all sat in their places. I made sure they were strapped in. Made sure the suits were on properly. Made sure they all remembered where the inflation buttons were. Then got into my own place and shouted, "Three, two, one . . ."

The suits began to hiss and grow, and we all swelled up like giggling tangerines again. The suits expanded into every corner of the module, with just our heads sticking out. Then the countdown started:

"Twenty . . . nineteen . . . eighteen . . ."

"I need a wee," said Hasan.

"Then do one. You've got your special suit on, don't forget."

"Pete Conrad wet himself just before *Gemini 5* took off," said Florida.

No one else heard her say this because there was a sound like mountains snoring. Everything shook like the worst earthquake film you've ever seen. Our stomachs dropped to the floor. The rest of ourselves dropped to the floor. And suddenly it felt like there really *was* a Giant Invisible Dad, but he was furious and he was crushing us between the palms of his hands. And we could do nothing because our arms wouldn't move. We couldn't shout. Because our faces wouldn't work.

And I remember thinking, If this is what it takes to get us up there, what is it going to take to get us down again?

Themoonyouidiot

Imagine you've scrunched up a piece of paper in one hand, then you open your hand and the paper opens up like a flower. That's what takeoff feels like.

But soon we began to level off. Florida said, "Are we there yet?"

Then Max said, "Are we there yet?"

And soon they were all saying, "Are we there yet? Are we there yet?"

I tried to shush them in case there was an important message from DraxControl. Then there was a *ding dong* sound in my headset and a nice reassuring voice in my ear said, "Hello, Mr. Digby. My name is Li. I'm your flight controller for today."

"Nice to meet you, Li."

"You too. Any questions, just ask me. Right now you can relax. If you like, you can deflate your takeoff outfits and enjoy the weightless environment."

I said, "Crew, you may now deflate your escape suits." They all yelled, "Yay!" and I felt not just dadly but actually captainish.

We started to float around the cabin, propelled by the air from the deflating suits. In zero gravity we really were like a family of novelty balloons.

Last time we were weightless it had only lasted a couple of minutes. So this time we bobbed about enjoying it, waiting for it to stop. But it didn't stop. Max did ask me if it was time to start our first task. I said, "Soon." I was too happy being a balloon to bother being the grown-up just then.

A few minutes later the reassuring voice spoke in my ear again. "Mr. Digby," it said, "we have a glitch. The release for the protective shield hasn't worked. There is an override button on the multifunctional display. It's a black button, in the top right-hand corner. Can you see it?"

I could.

"If you could press that when I tell you."

This was completely cosmic. Something had gone wrong and I was putting it right. I didn't mention it to the others. I didn't want to panic them. The voice said, "Now." I pressed the button.

There was a sound like a door shutting somewhere far

away. The capsule rocked a little bit. Then everything went bright.

Our protective outer panels had blown away. Now we had windows. We could see the rejected panels tumbling away from us into space.

"Great job, Mr. Digby," Li's voice crackled in my ear. "Every mission has one glitch. You've just had yours. Now take it easy and enjoy the view."

The view by the way was Earth.

Not all of it, not to start with. Less than a quarter of it. We were still so close that that quarter filled the window. Because we were high up, I thought we'd be looking down. But really it felt more like looking up. And all we could see was blue. It was completely the bluest ever blue, except for bands of cloud and veins of green on the surface of the sea. We were looking at the southern Pacific.

Max was thrilled by the rejected safety panels. "Look at them go!" he yelled. "They're like torpedoes!"

I said, "I did that."

"What?"

"When DraxControl tried it, it didn't work. I had to press a special button."

"Did you really," said Florida, adding, "Dad?"

"Next time," growled Max, "it's my turn."

"No," said Hasan, "next time it's my turn."

In their heads we were an X-Wing Fighter and the Earth was the Death Star. In all our heads the whole thing was so cosmic it had to be a game.

I discovered that if I pushed my feet against the wall, I could flit clear across the cabin, spin round and kick off again from the opposite wall, like Spider-man flying around New York. Then Florida popped up in front of me, making a buzzing sound with her mouth, and miming a few passes with an imaginary lightsaber.

Looking back on it, I should have focused more on being dadly at this point. Because that's when DraxControl came on, asking for us to move on to our task. "You have a two-minute window to complete the task. Please commence now."

All we had to do was press the right buttons in the right order, then we'd be set for the trip home. Hasan and Max were still arguing about it. Samson Two put his hand up and said, "Please, sir, I'd also like to press the button," which was enough to get both Hasan and Max shouting at him. Maybe I should have just done it myself, but I was loving being a floaty Super Mario Matrix Jedi Power Ranger. Which is why I said, "Let's settle it with light-sabers!" and took a buzzing swipe at them. They ducked and then bobbed up again, looking a bit confused. I realize now that they'd probably never seen *Star Wars*. They'd definitely never seen a dad trying to make a crucial life-or-death decision with an imaginary lightsaber.

I shouted, "LUKE, I AM YOUR FATHER."

Florida thought this was hilarious and shouted, "You are NOT my father."

"And you are not Luke."

We were buzzing and laughing and laughing and buzzing. Then Max noticed Hasan was closing in on the buttons. He yelled, "Hey! He's cheating!" and went after him. Samson Two dived in underneath them. Next thing, they were pulling and shoving each other in front of the multifunctional displays.

And the next thing after that: a long screeching noise. Then a jolt, as though we'd been caught on a bungee. Then we spun round. And round. And round. And over and round. Fast. And random. Like the cage of the Cosmic.

And a light strobed off and on and off like blue lightning.

And somewhere in the middle of it the voice of Drax-Control was shouting in my ear.

Then it stopped.

Then it shouted.

Then it stopped again.

The Earth vanished.

And then came back.

Then vanished.

And then came back.

And then we stopped rolling.

And Earth was gone.

No one said a word.

We drifted over to the window and pressed our faces against the glass, looking for some sign of it.

It was very quiet. And very dark. And very, very scary.

It didn't take Samson Two long to work out what had happened. The buttons had been pressed in the wrong order. The *Dandelion*'s protective cover had blown off and its silvery sails had popped out. But it had not separated from the command module.

The solar sails had opened unexpectedly—that was the metallic screeching noise—and immediately picked up a gust of solar wind. The sails were designed to push the *Dandelion* gently forward. But our command module was still stuck to the top of the *Dandelion*. Instead of gliding off nicely toward the moon's orbit, the *Dandelion* had gone spinning over on its side and pulled us off course. The sails weren't acting like sails on a ship; they were more like the sails on a windmill, spinning us round and round. And it was taking us with it.

We couldn't see the Earth out of the window. But we

did see a thing that looked like a satellite dish go by, and something like an aerial. Our satellite dish. And our aerial. Which was when I realized I couldn't hear DraxControl in my earpiece anymore. All our communications equipment had snapped off.

They all started yelling and blaming each other and pushing and shoving. Pushing and shoving under weightless conditions is more long-winded than it is on Earth. You push someone and it takes them a few minutes to get back to you with a shove.

I was going to join in when I noticed a message window flashing on the monitor. A message. Maybe we'd be all right after all.

The message was "Permanent Fatal Errors."

I could still hear them fighting and shouting behind me. I was going to yell too—something like, "We are now completely doomed and it's totally all your fault!" But when I turned to face them they were all looking at me. Like I would know something.

Like I would know what to do.

Like I was their dad.

Like the end would never come as long as I was there.

"Is there a message?" said Samson Two.

"Yes."

"What does it say?"

I could've told him, "The message is 'Permanent Fatal Errors'. So we're dead. And by the way, I'm not a dad. I'm a kid. So stop looking at me like that."

These children—Hasan, Samson Two, Max—their dads weren't looking out for them at all. Their dads made them do all this stuff to make them cleverer or richer or more successful. And then they'd been packed off to Doom in Space. But still they thought someone, somewhere would be looking out for them.

In the circumstances, it felt like that should be me.

I thought, okay, you lot are my mission. I am Engaged. I turned off the monitor and said, "Everything's going to be okay. We just need to find Earth and then we'll go back home."

Florida hadn't noticed till then. Now she screamed, "Ohmygod, the Earth has gone! What have you done with the Earthyouidiot!?"

"It hasn't gone. It's just not very visible at the moment. Don't worry, it'll turn up."

"How do you know?" said Samson Two. "What if it doesn't?"

"Because all my . . . all Florida's stuff is there: the Playmobil Viking ship, the slightly leaky Super Soaker, the 'It's Your Solar System' glow-in-the-dark mobile . . ."

I don't know what made me start listing stuff. But it

worked. It reminded them about the Earth. How real and big it was. It made them see it in their heads and they started adding things to the list until they calmed down and finally went to sleep.

The bright blue sleeping bags are attached to the wall. Hanging there, with their heads lolling, the children look like they're sleeping in a row of Christmas stockings. And I'm the only one awake, like I'm Father Christmas or their guardian angel or something.

And just now the cabin suddenly filled with light. It came flooding in like water. Sunlight.

The thing is, if there is all this sunlight coming in, which wasn't coming in before, that means that until now the sun was behind something. And that can only be the Earth. Can't it?

The Earth—I still can't see it, but now I know it's there.

I closed the filter on the observation window. I didn't want the kids to wake up yet.

There's a hatch in the floor just in front of the multi-functional displays, the hatch that leads to the *Dandelion* module. I thought I'd go down there and look through the *Dandelion*'s windows. I might even be able to see the Earth from there.

I fiddled with the catch. It was simple enough. It was only

when it was actually moving I suddenly thought, What if it doesn't lead to the *Dandelion*? What if it goes straight to the outside, to the wastes of space? If it does, we'll all be sucked out by the pressure differential and our heads will explode.

Luckily that didn't happen.

Inside the *Dandelion* it was surprisingly unrockety. Three rows of seats, two massive windows. It really was like being inside an unusually spacious ice-cream van. The good news was there was a lot—cupboards full—of food and drinks.

The bad news was that—even with those massive windows—you still couldn't see the Earth.

There was a massive thing between us and the sun, but it wasn't the Earth.

Something moved behind me.

Florida. She had come down into the ice-cream van. Then "Oh. My. God," she said, pointing out of the window. "Do you know what that is?"

I nodded and said, "I think I may have seen it before."

"That," said Florida, "is themoonyouidiot."

An Unscheduled Diversion

When you look at the moon from Earth, it looks a bit smudgy. I mean, you know the smudges are mountains and so on but really they just look like blotches. But from where I'm sitting, you can see they're mad, spiky storybook mountains. The surface is white as paper and the shadows are sharp and definite. It's like looking at the map of an imaginary realm in a Warcraft manual. Massive mountains, deep valleys, empty plains. All it needs is a few trolls and dragons and a big fancy compass.

"What?" yelled Florida. "What is the moon doing there?"

I said calmly, "Oh, you know—orbiting the Earth, affecting the tides, stuff like that." It's important for a parent to stay calm in all eventualities.

Inside my head, my panicky twelve-year-old voice was screaming, "It's pulling us nearer and nearer. It's pulling us into orbit. That's what it's doing. We're going to be left circling the moon forever. What are you going to do?"

The truth is, I had been hoping that when I got into the *Dandelion*, there would be some brakes and a steering wheel and I'd be able to stop us, change direction—maybe do an intergalactic three-point turn—and drive us home. But there didn't seem to be any controls at all.

Florida shrugged and said, "I suppose we'll just have to take a free-return trajectory round the moon to bring us back."

I said, "Sorry?"

She said, "You know, like on *Apollo 13*?"

Calm Dad Voice (out loud): "Yeah. Exactly. That's exactly my plan. What you just said."

Scared Little-Boy Voice (inside): "What did she say? Is she saying there's a way out of this?"

Florida plonked herself down on one of the bench seats and growled, "I hate it when this happens. When you think you're nearly home and then the bus goes off on some . . . what's it called?"

"Trajectory?"

"No, you know, when you catch the 81, it comes right up to the overpass and you think, I'm nearly home, and then it goes off *under* the overpass, round the island and all the way up to the 24-hour Tesco before it comes back to where it was when you were nearly home."

"Oh yeah."

She crossed her arms and stared out of the window. She really did look like she was sitting on the number 81. I sat down next to her and said, "Yeah. Trajectories, eh—don't you hate them? How do they work . . . exactly?"

And then she told me the whole story of *Apollo 13.* Which is this: *Apollo 13* was on its way to the moon when one of its oxygen tanks blew up. The crew climbed into the little tiny landing module and used it as a kind of life raft. Then they flew right round the back of the moon so that the moon's gravity would give them a bit of extra speed and—by burning their remaining engine at the right time—broke their orbit and made it home to Earth.

Obviously that's a summary. In Florida's version there was a lot about whether thirteen really is an unlucky number and which Hollywood actors played the astronauts in the film version—Kevin Bacon and Tom Hanks, by the way—and who those actors are married to now.

While she was talking the others must've noticed the open hatch in the floor of the command module. One by one they floated down into the *Dandelion.* The first one in was Hasan, who didn't seem to notice the moon at all. He spread himself out on one of the bench seats saying, "It's much more comfortable down here."

Samson Two stared out of the window with his mouth open until Florida said sarcastically, "Yes, it's the moon. We've got to go right round the back of it. Can you believe it?"

"The moon? But . . . no one said anything about the moon."

"It's a diversion," said Florida. "An unscheduled diversion."

"But . . . the moon? It's so far away."

"Not anymore," said Florida.

The real problem was Max. It wasn't the moon that bothered him; it was the *Dandelion*. "Our mission was to decouple this module, to put it in orbit. We must do it now."

I explained that we couldn't do it right this minute because we had a problem.

"Not to release it means we've failed. Failure is not an option."

"We haven't failed. We just haven't succeeded—yet. We'll press the green button when we can."

"But Dr. Drax said—"

"Dr. Drax didn't know."

"She knows more than you do. I am now going to press the green button," he said.

I ran after him. Weightless running isn't exactly speedy. It felt like one of those dreams where you're trying to get away from mad dogs but your feet are sort of stuck to the floor. In the end I sort of toppled forward into an involuntary somersault, just caught him with my foot and sent him spinning back toward the seats.

I grabbed the hatch myself and said, "Listen, we've got a plan and it's a plan about . . ." What was it about? "Florida is going to tell you what it's about."

Delegation, see. Very important with teenagers.

"I haven't got any plan," said Florida.

Delegation and affirmation.

"You've got a brilliant plan, Florida. About trajectories, remember?"

"Oh. The free-return trajectory," said Florida. "Like on *Apollo 13*. You must remember *Apollo 13*?"

"The brilliant failure," said Samson Two. "The lunar mission that was supposedly abandoned because of a faulty oxygen tank." I didn't notice him saying "supposedly" at the time, but I certainly noticed it ten minutes later.

She explained the whole thing to them about going round the back of the moon until we were facing the right way, and she pointed out that it was going to be easy for us. It was going to be a ride, in fact. "On *Apollo 13*, all they had was this tiny module and it was really cramped and there wasn't enough oxygen or power. We've got this whole solar-powered *Dandelion* and it's got plenty of room and loads of food. So . . . it's a picnic really. By comparison. The *Dandelion* is meant for space travel but not reentry. The command module is meant for reentry but not really for space travel. So we use the *Dandelion* to get us back to Earth orbit. Then we all go back into the command module and use that to get back to Earth. Understand?"

Everyone said yes. What was there not to understand? But Max said, "Yes, I understand. And now I am going to press the green button."

"What?! Have you been listening to anything we've been saying?"

"Yes, but I listened to Dr. Drax more."

"Anyway, you can't press the button," said Hasan, "because it's my turn."

And the two of them hurled themselves toward the hatch.

I shouted, "No one is pressing the green button! We'll all be killed."

Samson Two said, "Of course we won't be killed. You don't believe we're really in space, surely?"

Everyone stopped and stared at him.

"Of course we are not really in space. This is a trick Dr. Drax has played on us. If we open the door, we will find that we are in the middle of Infinity Park, same as always. In fact, I am going to open it now."

He kicked his feet on the back of the seat and floated off toward the airlock.

I was going to go after him when I realized I had to go after Max too. My brain tried to choose between being shot out of a spaceship and accelerating to death, or being set adrift for ever and ever in a space ice-cream van.

In that horrible moment I realized that the real danger wasn't the infinite vacuum of space, or the six million possible flaws in the rocket. The real danger was the children.

> *Remember, a teenager is barely in control of anything—not even his or her own body. You are in control of everything. If your teens are reacting irrationally or disproportionately to some little thing, it's up to you to try to work out what's really upsetting them.*
>
> *from* Talk to Your Teen

Max was upset because he's very fixated on success. To him, being halfway to the moon in an ice-cream van meant we were failures. He thought that if we jettisoned the *Dandelion* we'd be winners again.

As for Samson Two, he was upset because he'd totally flipped out.

Which is understandable. If I didn't have to look after the others, I'd flip out too.

All I had to do to sort Max out was show him that getting ourselves home in one piece after all the problems we'd had would be an even greater achievement than just doing what Dr. Drax had told us to. So I said to him, "You know, Max, after all our problems, getting home in one piece will be an even greater achievement than just doing everything that Dr. Drax said."

He said, "All our problems are Hasan's fault."

"No," said Hasan, "they're all your fault."

"You pressed the wrong button. Now I'm going to press the right one."

"I didn't press any button: you did."

"No, *I* didn't press any button. You did."

I said, "I'm the DADDY and I DECIDE who presses the buttons. And I have decided that whoever WINS my game presses it. WHEN I SAY SO."

"Wins?" said Max, suddenly interested. Like I said, every monster has its soft zone. Winning is Max's. "What game?"

Hmmm. Yes. What game?

It turns out that Hasan had a board game in his PiP. "This game," he said, "taught me to love money. And that's why I love it." The game was Monopoly. There really is no getting away from it. I suppose that's why it's called Monopoly.

Low-gravity Monopoly is better than the Monopoly you play round the kitchen table, in that it lasts only a few minutes. If you've got a magnetic travel set—like Hasan's—the pieces will stay on the board. And if you carefully keep hold of the money, that's okay too. The problem is the dice. You can throw the dice, but they won't actually land. They just drift off in random directions, dipping and swooping like genetically modified sugar cubes. And they never stop spinning.

The endless spinning really interested Samson Two. "Fascinating," he said. "There must be some way to harness the energy these dice create by spinning like this." Then, just in case I was starting to feel a bit relaxed, he added, "I wonder how Dr. Drax has achieved this effect. It really does feel as though we are weightless. You could almost believe you were really in space."

We did try throwing the dice on to a loop of Scotch tape that we stuck to one of the seats, but it didn't really work, and during the arguments about whether it was a six or not I spotted Max heading back to the command module.

I shouted, "What about rock, paper, scissors?"

None of them—except Florida—had ever played that. They were completely interested in it for about twenty minutes. The first ten minutes were taken up discussing *why* paper beats rock and whether anyone would ever really try to use scissors to cut a rock. I had a round with Max in which he played dynamite and I played scissors. Then in the next round, he played paper and I played scissors again. Scissors wins.

He said, "You played scissors last time and I destroyed them with my dynamite. How can you still have scissors when I destroyed your scissors?"

"Well, they're not destroyed forever. Just until the next round."

This game was obviously too abstract for Max. He went very red and started yelling, "This is madness. One of them must be destroyed or how can there be a winner? You can only have a winner if something is DESTROYED!"

When he shouted "destroyed" like that I nearly panicked. But I didn't. I just said, "Hide-and-seek, anyone?"

Weightless hide-and-seek sounds like a good idea, but it was a bigger mistake than rock, paper, scissors. Weightless hide-and-seek was what nearly killed us all.

I was it. I counted very loudly to forty while they all went and hid. For that forty seconds I sat back on one of the window seats and looked out at the moon. Then I shouted, "Coming, ready or not!"

I could actually hear Samson Two moving about under one of the chairs. It would've been a great hiding place, except for the weightlessness, which kept making him float up and bang his head. So I caught him and we both went looking for the others.

I could feel that Max was watching me. I looked up and glimpsed him holding on to the ceiling with his fingers, looking down at us, hoping that we hadn't seen him. I decided to let him stay there so that he could win, since winning was such a big deal for him.

I moved to the front of the *Dandelion*, between the front seat and the window, which is where I used to sit on the top deck of the bus to school. I noticed there was a bigger-than-you-really-needed space between the two front seats and a kind of groove in one of the floor panels. I gave it a tug and it rolled sideways. Florida was looking straight up at me, with this big grin on her face, saying, "Come and see. . . ."

I swung myself down there, and Samson Two followed me. Florida had found the driving cab of the *Dandelion*! Everything was there—a driver's seat with a proper steering wheel, even wing mirrors—so that you could see the solar sails properly. The view was a bit rubbish because the command module was still stuck on the front of it. But that only made it feel more like an ordinary car—a car stuck behind a big truck or something. A car that I could drive. I looked at Florida and she nodded at me. She'd read my mind.

"Except you're a rubbish driver," said Florida.

"Yeah, but it'll be easy up here. There's hardly any traffic."

"This is so disappointing," said Samson Two. "Doesn't feel a bit like a spaceship. It's just made from old bits of bus."

I couldn't help but sit down and try the seat. Florida said, "Be careful. We really need a manual. You never know—one of those things"—she waved a hand at the control panel—"might be the ejector button or something."

I looked up. There, just above the driver's seat, was one of those sun visors that you pull down, just like in a car. Dad keeps his manual, his road maps and his insurance on the back of his, fastened with an elastic band. I pulled it down. A sightseer's map of the moon, some insurance documents and . . . a manual. With a troubleshooting section, a "getting started" page, a diagram of the instrument panel and . . .

It was the diagram of the instrument panel that put the fear in me. The little drawings of the buttons seemed to jump off the page and shoot toward me like Death Guild spears. Buttons! The button! Max and Hasan were out of my sight. They could be dishing out nine different kinds of Doom right this second.

I pushed myself into the air and shot up through the hatch like Superman, banged my head on the ceiling of the minibus, somersaulted toward the command module, wriggled through the air lock and there was Max, standing right next to the green button, about to press it.

I have no idea how I got from the bottom of the module to the top so quickly. But I was between him and the button faster than I could think about it and the two of us were wrestling through the air, knocking into pipes and sleeping bags and handles and dials.

Florida got herself right next to the button and shouted, "So Hasan wins! Isn't that right, Dad?"

This caught Max's attention. "Hasan wins?"

I said, "Well, I can't see him—can you? Doesn't that make him the last to be found? That means he's the winner."

You could hear a little rumble of dissatisfaction brewing somewhere inside Max. I was half expecting him to put his head back and howl like a wolf.

Then I said, "Of course, if *you* find him, then you're the winner."

And he was off. I told Florida to stay and guard the green button while I went off with Max and Samson Two to find Hasan.

And here's the thing. We couldn't find him.

The command module—no sign. The *Dandelion*—no sign. The cockpit—no sign.

Hasan had gone missing.

In space.

The worst thing you can do with teens is get sucked into an argument on their terms. They have more time than you do. They can keep going forever.

from Talk to Your Teen

"Hasan is not on the rocket. Therefore, Logic says, he got off the rocket."

"Samson Two, you're always telling us what Logic says. Who is Logic—your imaginary friend? Why don't you say something yourself instead of letting Logic do all the talking."

"He left the rocket."

"Well, Logic says you can't leave a rocket. Because it's in space."

"Logic says if someone leaves a rocket—which Hasan has—then the rocket isn't in space. It's a simulation."

We searched the rocket again.

We didn't find him.

Florida said, "You know, there was this television program once where everyone thought they were in space and it turned out they were in Essex or something."

"I know."

"And then," said Samson Two, "what about the Apollo space program, where they managed to convince everyone they'd been to the moon?"

Max said, "They never went to the moon!? Are you sure?"

Florida said, "Of course they went to the moon. Mr. Bean went to the moon. We talked to him about it."

"Well, I hate to call anyone a liar," said Samson Two, "but if they went to the moon, why did they never go back?"

"Oh, people always say they're going back and they never do," I said. "My parents went to Spain on holiday once. They said they were going to go back every year, but they never did."

Samson Two was not going to let go of this. "Have you seen the picture of the American flag on the moon? The flag is flying, isn't it?"

"Yes."

"Well, there's no wind on the moon. So how would the flag fly? It's an obvious fake."

I said, "Maybe, just maybe, the people who went all the way to the moon knew there was no wind up there so maybe, just maybe, they put a little bit of wire in the top of the flag to make it stick out. After all, they did build a whole load of rockets with six million moving parts each so maybe, just maybe, they actually thought of putting wire in flags."

Samson Two didn't even blink. "Logic," he said, "says just open the door and see."

"Okay, Logic. Why not do that? Go on, Logic."

"I will."

"I didn't say you; I said 'Logic'."

"Logic says I'll do it."

"No, Logic says I'll do it. I'm in charge. I'm the one responsible. I'll go outside."

Why did I say that?

Going outside a rocket in space is called EVA—extra-vehicular activity. Unfortunately I'd missed the part of training where we did that because of Eddie Xanadu's electric Ribena. The others remembered the important things—how to put the helmet on, how to connect your oxygen, how to check the EVA suit. There was a section in the manual about how to open the airlock. And suddenly there I was, ready to go into space. I was standing inside the airlock and Florida was pointing to a coiled yellow rope. "That's the safety harness," she said. "It ties you to the rocket so you don't just drift off. Put it on straightaway. You're dead without that."

I fastened myself into the safety harness. Florida sealed

the inside door behind me, and for a minute I was bobbing by myself inside the airlock. It was like standing in a lift. It seemed so ordinary—apart from the fact that I was levitating—that I started to think that maybe Samson Two was right. Maybe we weren't in space. Maybe we were in some kind of simulation. Then the external door started to open. There was just a slant of black at first. Black so solid that it looked like a wall. It was hard to believe that things could move around in it. Then I started to see the underside of one of the *Dandelion*'s silver sails. I'm saying now that's what it was, but it was hard to tell. It was so dazzling that you couldn't really make out the shape. It blazed like the filament of a really strong lightbulb. Then the door opened wider. And I was out there in the black nothingness. Floating free.

Suddenly I collided with one of the sails and rolled around under it until I hit one of the struts and something made me grab hold of it. I hung there like a kind of mad Christmas decoration and for a second or two it was completely the most cosmic thing ever. The huge moon was in front of me and my feet seemed to be dangling in a kind of milky bath of stars. In a moment I was going to turn myself round and see if I could see the Earth. Meanwhile I was enjoying how intense it all was. The space between the stars was blacker than anything I'd ever seen. But everything that was shining—the sail, the moon, the stars, my metal cuffs—was shining a million times brighter than you've ever seen anything shine. Even my yellow safety cord seemed to shine. I remember hanging there watching it slither through my legs and snake off into space. I remember thinking, Hey, I've got a safety cord; I can let go. And at the same moment thinking, If one end of it is fastened to me, what's the other end fastened to?

Nothing.

It was just drifting off into space.

I'd fastened myself to the cord, but I had not fastened the cord to the module.

All I can remember after that is my own hands. My own hands gripping the struts, trying to hold on. My own hands shuffling painfully slowly along the sail toward the module. I thought about going hand over hand, like on monkey bars, but I was too terrified to let go with one hand even for a second. It seemed to take hours to get back to the side of the rocket. I was sweating and my heart was thumping. By the time I was next to the rocket, my helmet was starting to steam up.

That's when I realized I wasn't really sure which way it was back to the hatch. I'd rolled over so many times under the sail, I couldn't remember now whether I came out of the back or the front.

I worked out that if the yellow cord was streaming past me, then it must be pointing in the opposite direction to the one I had come from. Also I knew I couldn't see the moon from the hatch, so the hatch must be at the end farthest from the moon.

Underneath the sail, there was a strut attaching it to the module. I edged down that and found the sill of the compartment the sails had been in before they popped out. I gripped that and followed it toward the back.

It took ages. By the time I got to the end, I was too tired to do anything except hang there, staring straight at a couple of rivets and a big metal panel. I knew the hatch must be nearby, but I couldn't see much by then because of the condensation in my helmet. I was also starting to worry about how much oxygen I had left.

I ran my hand over the panel until I came to the edge of it. There was a double row of rivets there, just wide enough to squeeze my fingers between. That should hold me for a second. I brought my other hand over and squeezed that in too. Then I reached out to find the next panel. Did the same. I was just clinging on by my fingertips the whole time.

I was crawling along the outside of something that was moving faster than a train.

I tried to find the hatch with my fingers. But suddenly my foot caught on something. It was stuck. I brought the other foot round to it. Yes! Two feet fitted inside. I ran one foot along the inside rim of whatever it was. Then I froze. The rim seemed quite sharp and metal. What if I ripped the suit? I stayed still for a while, trying not to breathe.

I was sure now that it was the hatch below me. I just wasn't sure how to get the rest of myself down there. I tried crawling down with my hands but keeping my feet tucked in. It only took me so far. I was going to have to try to jump down. But what if the moment I let go, I just shot off into space?

I had no choice. I had to risk it. I let go of the side of the rocket and at the same time, tried to push my legs inside as hard as I could. In my mind, this would make me slide elegantly, feet first, back inside the hatch. In fact, I banged my knees. The pain made me curl up into a little ball so for a second or two I was floating completely free in space. But the momentum of curling up made me turn right over and as I came round, I was passing the bottom of the hatch. I grabbed it and dragged myself inside. There was plenty to hold on to in there. I felt around blindly with my fingers and pressed a button. I could hear the airlock door closing behind me. I still wasn't out of danger. But I was so happy to be back inside I started to take my helmet off. I wasn't sure how to do it and fumbled around for a bit. When I finally got it off, I could see again. And the first thing I saw was the hatch door just clicking shut. If I'd known the proper way of undoing the helmet, if I'd got it off more quickly, the door would not have been fully closed and my head might have exploded, although I'd probably have suffocated first.

I stood with my forehead against the metal door. It felt so cool and so solid. I loved the way it didn't try to run away from me and leave me in space. It seemed like hours before the door opened—long, happy hours of just standing still, not gripping anything, not scared, appreciating the various properties of metal doorways.

As soon as the hatch opened, all the children were floating there in front of me, bobbing up and down like a bunch of cherubs. And they just looked so *alive*. I know it sounds mad, but I could see every one of their eyelashes. I wanted to count them. I could hear their breathing. I could hear eyelids opening and closing. Everything. It was like I'd completed a quest and all the rewards I'd earned—the health, the experience, the strength—were flooding into me. It was like I'd gained a superpower. Superhearing. I could've just stood and listened to them breathing and blinking all day. I wanted to hug them, to be honest, but obviously that would have been too weird.

Florida said, "Did you find him?"

"Who?"

"Hasan. You went outside to look for Hasan."

"No, he's not out there." I was so happy that I'd rescued myself, I'd forgotten about rescuing Hasan.

"What is out there?"

"Well, you know, the universe and stuff."

"If he's not out there, and he's not in here, where is he?" said Florida. "He can't just have vanished."

Max said, "First the Earth vanished and now Hasan has vanished. Everything keeps vanishing. Maybe we are going to vanish!"

I said, "Shh." Among all the new sounds I could hear—eyelids opening and closing, muscles and bones moving, electronic equipment buzzing, a counter from the travel Monopoly set hovering under the seats, I had noticed another sound—louder and rougher—coming from inside the wall, near the driving compartment. I floated over to it. To me it sounded deafening, but I knew that the others couldn't hear it at all. Because when I was looking for Hasan earlier, I hadn't heard it either. It was my new super-hearing that picked it up. I felt around on the wall for a bit and found a little gap between the panels. I pushed on one panel and tugged on the other, and there was Hasan, snoring.

He woke up, looking so pleased with himself. He said, "Did I win? When the soldiers came to my village I hid in a space behind the water tank for three days. I have had plenty of practice at hide-and-seek."

I said, "Of course. I forgot about that." It was strange to think that this might be only the second most dangerous game of hide-and-seek Hasan had ever played.

"So I won?"

"Yes. You won. You did really well."

"So," said Max, "he won. Finally I am a loser."

I looked at him. With my superhearing I could almost hear his heart beating faster than usual. Then it seemed to calm down. "You know," he said, "it does not feel so bad."

Florida shoved him and he floated backward all the way to the other side of the minibus. He laughed all the way. Watching him made me feel good. I knew then that the green button was finally safe from him.

I said, "Let's measure you all on the height chart. See if you've grown."

Florida looked at me like I'd gone mad. "You were only gone ten minutes. How would we have grown?"

"Space, isn't it? Like Samson Two said. Less gravity on your spine." They all lined up and I marked off their new heights next to the door, just like Mom used to do with me at home.

Samson Two said, "The power of suggestion is amazing. We've all grown an inch or so, just like we would've done if we were really in space."

"We are really in space," said Max. "Mr. Digby went outside, remember?"

"Yes," said Samson Two, "he went outside, read a newspaper and then came back inside."

I was tempted to say, "Okay then. If you don't believe me, *you* go out there." But I took a deep breath and said, "Okay. But you know, say it's only a simulation, we'll still need to know the proper altitude and the proper angle of departure to get the speed we need from our return trajectory. Can you work stuff like that out?"

"Maybe." He rummaged in his PiP and pulled out a book. A really old, thick book called *A Boy's Wonder Treasury of Science.*

"My mother gave this to me for my birthday one time," he said. "When I was small. It was *her* favorite book when she was small. Her mother had given it to her. It's old. I was ill for a while and had to stay off school. I sat in bed and read this book and it made me clever. I could feel it. It was like a magic power. It was a pity really, because I got so clever they sent me away to a special school and I did not see her so much after that. Still, sometimes when I am tired or when I do something not so clever, I sleep with it under my pillow and I can feel it making me clever again. That's how I know about the power of suggestion."

At the back of the book were these massive lists of numbers. Logarithmic tables. That's what they used to use to do complicated math before they invented calculators. "With this," said Samson Two, "I can work out the trajectory."

I said, "Well, if you need any help—I'm officially Gifted and Talented. And when we're ready and the time is right . . . we will, *all* of us, press that green button together."

They all cheered.

Florida suddenly shouted, "Look!"

Out of the window we could see a huge shadow moving across the moon like a carpet being rolled out.

"What is it?"

I knew what it was right away. I recognized it. I said, "That's the shadow of the Earth."

And we all watched it. It was the nearest any of us had come to seeing the Earth since we blew off course. It was the first time since then that we'd known for sure that the Earth was still there.

Except for Samson Two, obviously, who thought he was still in China.

The shadow scythed over the moon's surface, and I tried to imagine what bits of the Earth we were looking at.

Then I said, "Who's hungry?" and we raided the supplies of space food.

While we were all laying into Pork That Makes You Eat Your Own Hand, Florida suddenly burst out laughing and pointed at Max.

"What?" said Max.

"Look, he's talking to us, he's eating and he's weeing at the same time. You can see his waste bag pulsing."

"Max, are you weeing while we're eating?"

"Yes, I am."

"So am I," said Hasan.

And soon everyone was, except me. I didn't think it was dadly. I just stood and tutted a bit. I think that made it even more enjoyable for them. Hasan laughed so much he floated right up to the ceiling. Then Max did the same. And Florida and finally even Samson Two. They looked like some kind of giggly mobile, circling hilariously all over the ceiling.

It must've been just after that that we slipped into the shadow, and moved over the darkened surface of the moon.

Dark Side of the Moon

It's hard to believe in things you can't see. Things like gravity. I knew in my head that once we got nearer to the moon, the moon's gravity would just pull us in and make us go round the moon so that we were facing the right way. I knew that in my head. But I felt in my stomach that once we were past the moon, we might just keep going. And going. And going. Into Nothing.

And then the moon disappeared. I mean, it completely vanished. Florida started yelling, "It's gone! The moon is gone!"

And Hasan and Max threw themselves against the window, trying to spot it.

Samson Two carried on cheerfully working on his math. "Can't you see what's happened?" he said. "Obviously they've turned the simulator off. Great. It means they'll come and get us out of here soon."

Florida was right. Where the moon had been, it *was* totally black. But—maybe it was part of my new superpowers—I could see a pattern to the blackness. There was a huge curve where the stars were missing from the top right-hand corner of the window. As though there was something in between us and them. There was a great curve of darker darkness on top of the darkness. Like a bite taken out of the sky. I couldn't see the surface of the moon, but I could see its outline, where it blocked out the rest of the sky. It was like a puzzle. Once I could see it, I couldn't stop seeing it.

I pointed it out to the others. It took them a moment, but they all saw it in the end. And while they were looking, they all pressed against me, like I really was their dad.

It's very frightening, traveling along with this massive blackness next to you. It looks like a hole and it's hard not to believe that you're going to fall into it. We all stood looking at the forward edge of the crescent, because somehow that helped us remember that we would pass out of this darkness in the end.

Then suddenly, the edge started to glow—just a little at first—but getting brighter all the time.

"It must be the sun," said Florida.

But by the time she had finished saying this, we could

all see what was causing the brightness. And it wasn't the sun.

It was the Earth.

The first time we'd seen it since we left orbit.

It was the size of a golf ball and too blue to be true.

Obviously we'd none of us ever seen the world from this angle. But we'd all seen pictures and now it looked just like that. Our Earth. Our home.

Then, in an instant, it changed shape. It went from a flat disc to a ball. It seemed to go *pop*, like if you've ever had a badge and squeezed it in on itself, then let it pop back to shape. And then there it was, not a photograph anymore, our planet—and we were heading toward it.

I'd always wanted to see the world. And now I was—all in one go.

Doing the Dadly Thing

There's something about the way the Earth just sits there in the middle of all that blackness, with nothing holding it up, that makes you worry about it. I kept thinking that if I looked away it might just fall. I was so busy keeping the planet up that I completely forgot about Samson Two until he suddenly said, "Okay, well, we could go now."

"Go where?"

"If we burn one of the engines for eleven minutes, that will push us out of the moon's orbit and shoot us off toward the Earth."

I said, "We don't have engines. This is a solar-powered *Dandelion*."

Samson Two was flicking through the manual. "We have two retros and two thrusters. For burning out of orbits and for backing out of trouble. We could use them now or—"

"Or what?" Go to Tesco?

"Or . . . we could go round the moon one more time."

"Why would we want to do that?"

Samson Two looked up from the manual. "If we stayed in orbit but dropped down to a lower altitude, of say sixty-eight miles, that would give us greater velocity, so we'd leave orbit faster. Then, if my calculations are right, Earth would be some ten thousand miles nearer by the time we'd been round again, so we wouldn't have so far to go. So by adding the extra speed, and the shorter distance, we wouldn't lose much time by going round and we would be on a more beneficial flight path. They really are good, these logarithmic tables."

So we did another lap of the moon.

The first time, because of the angle and the shadow and so on we'd barely seen the lunar surface. This time, as we passed only sixty-eight miles above it, we felt as if we could see every boulder and rock. I got the spotter's guide down from behind the sun visor and pointed out the famous bits—the Sea of Tranquility, where Neil Armstrong made his giant leap (Samson Two snorted at this), the Fra Mauro formation, where *Apollo 13* had been meant to land, and the Sea of Storms, where Alan Bean camped. I said, "You know someone who has walked down there. That bit there, see?"

"Ridiculous," said Samson Two.

"There's no footage of it because he broke the TV camera," said Florida.

"How convenient," said Samson Two.

"He was the fourth man to walk on the moon. The third was his friend Peter Conrad. And you know what Alan said? He said part of him never came back. He said he wakes up in the night sometimes and thinks he's back there. And sometimes when something big is happening at home, he feels like he's watching it from up here. Like the Alan Bean you met on Earth is an avatar in a game and the real Alan Bean—the one controlling him—is up here."

I looked back at the others. They'd gone so quiet I thought they must be really impressed, but they were all playing on their Wristations.

When we were back on the dark side of the moon again we all had the same feeling of nervousness and dread we'd had the first time. We watched the edge of that curved absence where we knew the moon was, waiting for something to appear. And then something did.

Earth again. Home.

"Okay, are we ready for the burn?"

"Twenty-nine minutes to go, according to me," said Samson Two. "If we burn the engines for eleven minutes, we will be on our way home."

"How do we know you're right?" said Max.

"I have never been wrong before," shrugged Samson Two. "Not about math."

"And if you are wrong, what happens?"

"Well, it would be unlikely that we would miss Earth's gravitational field completely, but we might get caught in a very wide orbit. Too far out for us to reenter safely. We'd become a satellite of Earth, I suppose. Like a lot of space debris. Or a comet. Maybe if a comet went by we might get caught in *its* gravitational field and—"

"Stop talking!" yelled Max. "Can't you see you're scaring us to death?"

"It's only a simulation," said Samson Two.

The worrying prospect of being dragged around the solar system forever on the back end of a comet was what motivated my genius idea. I said, "Max, give me your Wristation."

"What for? You have your own."

"Yes, but mine has Professional Golfer on it. Yours has Orbiter IV. And somewhere in the menus there must be a free-trajectory flight simulation. If we play it using the specifications for the *Dandelion*—which are all here on the inside cover of the manual—then we'll be able to find out if our figures are right or not. If we play it in parallel with our real trip, then we can choose 'burn engines' and if it says, 'Good call,' we know we're okay and we can burn engines, and if it says, 'Uh-oh, you're dead—'"

"Then we're dead."

"Only in the simulation. In real life we don't do anything till we get top marks in the simulation."

"That," said Samson Two, "is genius."

"Not genius." Florida beamed at me. "Just Gifted and Talented."

So Samson Two set up the Wristation and played Orbiter IV, and I copied every move he made, dropping the *Dandelion* down to just the right altitude, holding her steady, getting her ready for the burn.

I told Max to prepare. "You can start the burn."

"I don't want to."

"What?! But you and Hasan fought each other for this job."

"Let Hasan do it then. I don't want to go back there."

"Back where?"

He pointed to Earth.

"Earth? Come on. How can you not want to go back to Earth?"

"It's better here."

"How is it better here? This is deep space."

But before he could answer, Hasan said, "It *is* better here."

And even Samson Two said, "It's an unexpectedly enjoyable simulation. I really enjoy the weightlessness effects."

"I like playing," said Hasan. "I like the hide-and-seek and

rock, paper, scissors. I like laughing about weeing. . . ."

"It's good here," said Max, "because there's only us. No one telling us to win, or smile, or study or earn money."

"Or shooting at us," said Hasan.

"What about my dad? He's a grown-up," said Florida loyally.

"But he's not like other grown-ups," said Samson Two. "He's different. I don't know why."

I really wanted to tell him. I wanted to say, "I'm a child too." But I didn't. I did the dadly thing. I let him go on believing.

And I took them round the moon again. And again. Round and round. As if the moon was a fairground ride.

And now I'm here in this command module all on my own. Where are the others? I'll tell you. I'll tell you because I'm feeling really proud of us all. I'll tell you even though you're never going to believe me. I know that even if we do get back alive, Dr. Drax is going to deny everything—plus we've signed forms promising to keep the whole thing secret.

The only way anyone will hear this recording and know what we've done is if we all die on reentry but this phone is somehow recovered from the wreckage.

If that happens, I think I'd quite like my dad to know what we did.

Because the thing is, the others are down there, on the moon.

Logic Says . . .

After our third lunar orbit, they still didn't want to go back to Earth.

I said, "Look, we'll have to go back in the end."

"Why? We've got food. We've got lots of food," said Hasan.

"But not a lifetime's supply. Anyway, Earth is your home. You have to go back." I was thinking about the Little Stars drama club, proper food, Mom and Dad.

"When we get back," said Florida quietly just to me, "I won't have a dad."

I looked at them all. "You can't spend your life up here."

The moment I said it I remembered Alan saying that in a way he *had* spent his life up here. That his memories of the moon were so bright and vivid that the things he did on Earth seemed gray by comparison. And I thought how completely cosmic it would be if I could fix that for them.

If I could make it so that part of them was always up here. So that when they were back on Earth and their dads were yelling and pushing them on, they could just tune out and come back up here, where—in their brightest memories—they would always be kids.

I got Samson Two to run a simulation on Orbiter IV. Basically, the *Dandelion* can't land anywhere. It's supposed to stay in space until it falls apart. But the command module is designed to touch down in the desert. And Dr. Drax's health-and-safety policy—Massive Overprovision—means that there's two of everything—two sets of retro-engines, two sets of parachutes, twice as much fuel as you'd need. The only thing there wasn't two of was the heat shield. But then that was there to protect you entering Earth's atmosphere and you wouldn't need that for a lunar descent because there isn't any atmosphere.

"Logic says it's possible," said Samson Two. "Of course, if you used half the fuel, you wouldn't have any spare. It's a calculated risk."

He seemed cool about it. But then he did think that the whole thing was a simulation.

We projected the Wristation simulation onto the wall so that we could all watch the command module floating down toward the moon, then plopping down onto the lunar surface in a shower of dust.

Seeing it happen on the wall made you feel as though it had already happened in some way.

Florida said, “Can we really do that? Let’s do it. Let’s do it. Let’s do it now.”

“The simulation is based on a two-hour schedule,” said Samson Two. “It would be feasible for the duration of one orbit. We’d have to redock with the *Dandelion* and use that to get back to Earth’s orbit.”

“Could you redock?”

“Well, the command module and the *Dandelion* are stuck together now. If we can unstick them, we should be able to restick them. But . . . someone would have to stay on board the *Dandelion* to guide it in.”

“Just like they did on the *Apollos*,” said Florida.

“Allegedly,” said Samson Two.

She said, “Well, that should be you then, Samson Two. Because you don’t think there’s anything out there anyway.”

“I’d be very interested to see how far the simulation goes,” said Samson Two.

I said, “I’ll stay. I can spend the time you’re down there practicing the redocking procedure on the Wristation. I’ll be genius at it by the time you come back.”

Max was worried. He said, “There should be an adult down there to supervise.”

I said, “No, the adult should be up here, keeping the place

nice for when you get home. You don't want a grown-up down there spoiling things. It should be kids only. With the dust and everything, it'll be like a giant sandpit."

"It's a crazy idea," said Hasan.

Florida was beginning to scowl.

I said, "But you've come all this way. A quarter of a million miles. Surely it would be *really* crazy not to go the last sixty-eight. And Max, this is your chance to press the green button. And Florida, you'll like it when you get there."

So I packed them off into the command module with their helmets and their space snacks, and some drinks, as though they were going to the beach. Florida was the last through the hatch. As she closed it, I said, "Hey, before you go, take these. Tell me what it's like, waterfighting on the moon." I gave her a few of the little rocket-shaped bottles of water.

They climbed into the command module, sealed the hatch behind them and pressed the green button. I felt the whole *Dandelion* sort of jump backward. Like it had hit a wall. It took a few minutes, but in the end it stabilized and, when it did, someone spoke to me! The unmistakable voice of Keira Knightley said, "Hi. We realize you had a choice of attractions today and we'd like to thank you for choosing the *Dandelion*."

I nearly jumped out of my spray-on suit.

It turned out that separating from the command module activated the Welcome System, so all these safety announcements played and then *Pirates of the Caribbean* started running on a plasma screen in the wall.

I watched it for a bit, but to be honest I preferred watching the stars through the window. And then the *Dandelion* moved on to the dark side again and the picture sort of digitized, froze, then vanished.

This was my fifth time round the back of the moon. I was in a lower orbit now so I suppose in a way I wasn't as far away as I had been the other times, but it felt farther.

A lot farther.

Because I was alone.

Everyone else, I mean *everyone* else—the other kids, Mom, Dad, Dr. Drax, the entire populations of China and America and Africa and Russia, children, grown-ups, old people, people shopping, eating, sleeping, being born, dying, even people who've been dead for hundreds of years like Tutankhamen—they were all Somewhere Else. I was the only human being on the far side of the moon.

Each time we'd gone round before, we'd spent the whole time looking at the blank space where the moon was. This time I looked out. And there were the stars. There's no point trying to describe them. It would be like trying to describe the molecules of oxygen you're breathing. There are too many of them.

The space between Earth and moon, that's space. Because it's a space between things. But on the other side of the moon, that's not space. I'm not between anything. This is the universe. I feel like I'm seeing it all, every bit of it. And it is big.

There are more stars than there are people. Billions, Alan had said, and millions of them might have planets just as good as ours. Ever since I can remember, I've felt too big. But now I felt small. Too small. Too small to count. Every star is massive, but there are so many of them. How could anyone care about one star when there are so many spare? And what if stars were small? What if all the stars were just atoms in something even bigger? What if stars were just pixels? And Earth was less than a pixel? What does that make us? And what does that make me? Not even dust. I felt tiny. For the first time in my life I felt too small.

The *Dandelion* was filling up with light. The stars were getting just a bit dimmer. Like someone was drawing a curtain over them. But I knew what was behind the curtain now. Behind the curtain was everything, and I was nothing. What was the point in even trying to find the others? What was the point in anything? I felt my hand grip the wheel. But I didn't know which way to turn it. How could anything I did make a difference? And if I asked for help, who would hear me?

Then my phone *ping*ed. I had a text: "Welcome to

DraxUniversal, the first truly universal network."

And just after that it rang.

I answered it. A voice said, "Liam, where are you, son?" It was my dad.

"Well, I'm . . . Is this you, Dad?"

"Of course it's me. I've been ringing you for days. Ever since you rang us. Your mom was worried about you. She thought you sounded upset. And she was worried that they were letting you stay up so late. Where are you, by the way? This is a great signal."

"It's a new network."

I was still looking back toward the massive empty universe. But I was talking to my dad and suddenly everything was different. My dad's voice was real. The stars were just . . . decoration.

"Are you okay? Because if you're not, I'll come and pick you up."

"I'm okay. Anyway, it's a bit far."

"Doesn't matter how far it is. I'm your dad. If you want me to pick you up, just say so."

I was going to say something but then he said, "Did you see the match last night? I think they're developing a real attitude problem. They go one–nil down and they just fall to pieces. Did you find that St. Christopher, by the way?"

"Yes. Thanks."

"Don't forget to bring it home. My dad gave it to me. He's not a saint anymore, St. Christopher, but anyway . . . he's looked after me. You know the story, don't you?"

I did. St. Christopher was some kind of giant superhero who used to carry travelers across a river, and one day this toddler turned up and asked him to carry him. St. Christopher popped him on his shoulders and carried him, but the toddler kept getting heavier and heavier and heavier until St. Christopher nearly drowned. It turned out the toddler was Jesus, so when St. Christopher was carrying him, he was carrying, well, the world. It was a story about gravity really.

"I bet it's nice in the Lake District this morning. I bet you've got a nice view, eh? What can you see?"

I said, "I've got a great view." I could see the Earth. And lovely as the stars had been, the Earth was . . . you could see it was special. It was bright blue, for one thing. For some reason—maybe it was because I was getting tired of being weightless—I thought about gravity. And how good gravity is. Not just because it keeps you on the ground. Even though that is good. I mean, I've loved being weightless, but it's like living on cotton candy. In the end you want potatoes. But it wasn't that.

It's gravity that keeps the gases round the Earth, the gases that we breathe, and it keeps the water in the oceans and the clouds in the sky, so that it never gets to be a hundred and thirty degrees on the surface. And it's gravity that keeps the sun together. If there was even a tiny bit more gravity than there is, the sun would be more compact and it would burn brighter and faster and it would only have lived a few million years so there would've been no chance for life to grow. And if there was even a bit less gravity, then the sun would burn too dim and the Earth would never have got warm enough for life.

"Are you on a main road?" It was Dad again.

"Not really. Well, yeah, in a way. . . ." In my head I was listing all the things that I could remember from Earth: Mom, Dad, Southport Fair, the 61 bus . . . and I put my thumb up to blot the Earth out again, but this time it didn't quite blot out and then I saw something—like a tiny mosquito, whizzing up over the top of my thumb, somewhere out there.

The command module was on its way back.

Dad said, "I tell you what . . . can you see a pub or a hotel or anything? Hang on. My credit's going here. Text me. I'll top up and use that DraxWorld thing to find you. Righto?"

And his phone went dead. Which was just as well, because the docking procedures take a bit of concentration.

I'm putting this phone away now till the children are back on board.

This Is Not a Simulation

Well, I did it. I successfully redocked the command module with the *Dandelion*. If it had been a game of Orbiter IV, I would have got an extra life for that.

The children came back through the hatch, giggling and pushing each other, and Samson Two said, "Guess what? You were wrong!"

"What?"

"This is not a simulation. We really are in space! We've just had a water fight on the moon." He went on to explain that water fighting on the moon turns out to be quite complicated.

You can squirt the water all right, but it flies this spooky, curved flight, like a diagram, following an arc toward the ground. And it doesn't ever find its target. In midflight it turns to tiny clouds and drifts along like ghosts for a while before disappearing altogether.

He said it was because they were in direct, unmediated

sunlight. The temperature could've been anything up to 266 degrees. The water just boiled.

I thought it must have been weird standing there, feeling quite comfortable but knowing that if you took your suit off you'd boil to death.

But they didn't.

They smelled slightly fireworky. This was because some elements of the moon dust they'd trailed in had reacted with the oxygen inside the *Dandelion*. And they were covered in the dust. Just covered. They looked like chimney sweeps. I found a little hoover for cleaning up crumbs attached to the wall near the food cupboards and I made them hoover their suits.

"Otherwise everyone will know what you did," I said. "They'll be able to tell by looking at you."

Max wanted to know why it was such a big secret. "Surely it's something to be proud of, being the first child on the moon?" he said.

And Florida said, "They're going to find out anyway, next time anyone goes there. D'you know what we did?"

"No," said Samson Two, "don't tell him. It's a surprise."

"Oh," said Max, "we almost forgot. A present. Moon rock."

And he gave me a square gray stone from another world.

* * *

What else did they do down there? Well, seeing as I'm the dad, I'll tell you like a dad would:

1. **How we got there.** We had a great run out. We didn't see any traffic to speak of. Just one meteor shower and that was it.
2. **What the parking was like.** For a start, the parking was completely free of charge. And there were an infinite number of parking spaces. As long as you looked out for the boulders and canyons. How come they can provide ample parking on the moon and not in Bootle, I'd like to know.
3. **What it was like in the old days.** Well, they had the Apollo program. There seemed to be some bloke going to the moon every few weeks. I thought we'd all be going there for our holidays when we grew up. Now look.
4. **Something thoughtful which it made you think.** We walked on the moon. We made footprints somewhere no one else had ever made footprints, and unless someone comes and rubs them out those footprints will be there forever because there's no wind.
5. **Something to do with last night's soccer.** No soccer because there wasn't enough gravity, but we had a water fight instead. The winner was—surface conditions.

After they were back on board we did one more orbit. Three-quarters of the way round, we burned the *Dandelion*'s boosters and we were heading back to Earth. They all rushed to the back to watch the moon getting smaller and smaller. Florida did ask me then, "What about you, Dad? Did you have a good time?"

"It was all right."

It might look like a coincidence that Dad rang me just as the phones came on. But it wasn't. He'd been trying for days and days. He got through the moment they came back on because he'd been trying all the time—that's what dads do. I had to look out for the children, like Dad looked out for me and his dad had for him, right back through time. Dadliness was out there among the stars, a force like gravity, and I was part of it.

But in the end, Florida's obsession with weight was what saved us.

"According to my math," said Samson Two, "we should begin reentry procedures now."

"You are joking," I said. "We're miles away."

When you do reentry on the simulator, the Earth feels like this giant wall right next to you. If we looked out of the window now, yes, it looked big, but you could still see the curve. You could tell you were way out.

"What you're saying is that my math is wrong. Which is simply illogical."

"What I'm saying is that it looks a bit far away. It looks a bit high. To be honest, I don't want to jump from here."

Florida said, "Samson Two, when you did your math, did you remember to add the weight of the *Dandelion*? Or did you do your calculations based on just the command module?"

Samson Two stared at her for a while and then said, "Excuse me, please." And started his math again.

So we're still in high orbit now. We're using the sails to glide down as gently as we can into a lower and lower and faster and faster orbit. It's like the world's biggest, gentlest spiral slide. With views of Greenland, the Pacific and Northern Russia.

"Can't we just keep going nice and gently like this till we get down?" said Hasan.

Sadly not. Eventually we started to see the glowing envelope of atmosphere. You can't just float through that. It's a firewall.

We're back in the command module now.

We've pressed the green button—all of us together this time. I felt the jolt as we uncoupled the *Dandelion*. I could almost hear Keira Knightley's voice kicking in: "We realize you had a choice of carrier today and we'd like to thank you for choosing . . ." as she drifted off into space.

* * *

We know what buttons to press to make our descent. We're just waiting for the right moment. The monitors are all still out. Samson Two is running Orbiter IV on the Wristation. We're all watching it on the wall. I'm pressing the real buttons a few seconds after he presses the game ones.

I gave them a team talk. I said, "Reinflate your Vehicle Escape Suits. And stay calm. I know we can do this, because we are cosmic."

Then I jettisoned the bottom half of the module—the bit with the window and the door and all those things that can't stand the pressure.

So now we are flying blind. We've got no window. I can more or less feel the angle in my bones. If we hit it wrong, we bounce off into space. Now the gravity is really hurting. It must be increasing. We must be right.

I'm looking at Dad's St. Christopher. It's rocking from side to side like there's an earthquake. I can feel myself getting heavier and heavier, like the boy in his story. I can barely move. The simulator is counting down. And now I can hear it saying, "Uh. Oh. You're. Dead."

We Got a Bit Lost

It was very quiet. Everything was white and cold. I was lying there, trying to figure out what was happening. I could feel something hot—breath: stinking, hot breath—and a smell of damp and the sound of breathing. I noticed all these things before I noticed where they were coming from—a wolf.

A wolf? I sat up and it snarled at me. More hot, stinking breath.

The door of the command module was open. There was snow outside and more wolves. Shoving each other, trying to get in.

We're back on Earth.

But we're tinned food.

Something went whizzing past my head and hit the wolf between the eyes. It yelped and backed off.

Florida lunged past me, lashing out at the wolf, and

pulling the hatch shut. She yelled, "I've just been to the moon and back in an ice-cream van. I'm not about to be eaten by a dog."

The "dogs" howled and scratched at the hatch. I said, "They're not dogs. They're wolves."

She passed out.

St. Christopher was in pieces on the floor. So that was what she threw at the wolf. I remember thinking Dad would go mad. He said it had really looked after him. Mind you, I suppose it's really looked after us.

I sat with my back to the door, keeping it pushed shut. That's when I noticed my Draxphone wedged into the multifunctional display unit. I dashed over, grabbed it, then threw myself against the door again. That's where I am now. No one is looking for us. I know this because Dr. Drax said she would deny all knowledge of us. But now I've got the phone, it doesn't matter. I can call Dad. I can tell him to get someone to find us.

I called Dad.

The phone rang twice. Then it beeped. A text. "You have no credit."

So now I'm sitting here, just talking to the phone. No one is listening. Even if someone knew we were out here, how would they find us? One little module the size of a Smart car, stuck out in the frozen wastes of Siberia, which is bigger than Europe.

The others are waking up. They're all bruised and bloody. They're glad to be alive, but they don't realize that being alive is only a temporary situation.

Wait. Got to stop. Got to stop talking because. Because my phone is ringing.

It was Dad. "Liam, it's me. I thought you were coming home today."

"Dad, hi, we got a bit lost."

"I know you're not in the Lake District, Liam. I know you're up to something. Just tell me where you are."

"Not sure."

"Okay. This is what you do: find a pub. . . ."

"A pub?"

"No. You're too young. What else comes up on DraxWorld? Libraries. Schools. Anything like that. Find one, call me back and I'll know where you are. I should be able to tell from the phone, but it's obviously gone wrong. It says you're in Waterloo, but you're not, are you?"

"Maybe. I mean I might be in *a* Waterloo."

"There's only one Waterloo, isn't there?"

"No, there's hundreds, Dad. One in Sierra Leone, one in Brussels, one in Brazil—"

"You're not going to tell me you're in Africa?"

"No, I don't think so. I might be in Siberia though."

"Very funny. Leave it with me. I'll sort something out."

He hung up. I looked at the others and said, "What happened? I thought we died."

"We forgot about the parachutes—again," said Samson Two, "but then Max pressed the button and saved us."

Max said, "No, Florida pressed the button and saved us."

Florida said, "No, Hasan pressed the button and saved us."

Hasan said, "No, Samson Two pressed the button and saved us."

"Maybe you all did."

My dad did sort everything out. It turned out I was wrong about Dr. Drax. Of course she was looking for us. She wanted to keep our trip a secret, so she wasn't going to leave a used spaceship lying around.

Dad's SIM card was a clone of mine, remember. So his phone logged my phone's position. And when I saved phone numbers, they saved onto his card as well as mine. That's how he was able to call Dr. Drax and give her our precise location.

That's why she turned up in her plane a couple of hours later with blankets and drinks and hot food and a lot more forms to fill in.

She was very nice to us. Then she said, "And, Mr. Digby, I believe you have a phone. Hand it over. And any cameras, diaries . . . anything that proves where you've been."

Special Gravity

So where am I now? Well, I'm in the New Strand Shopping Center, sitting by the water fountain while Mom and Dad are in Switched-On Electricals upgrading his satnav. I've borrowed my dad's phone so I can play Snake on it while I'm waiting for them. And while I'm noodling around, looking for the game, I notice that his audio diary is nearly full. And that's when I realize. Our phones were twins. When I reentered the atmosphere, my space diary was saved to his card, down here in Bootle, too. So I can listen to it all again.

And I can tell you how it ends.

The best thing about being on Earth is definitely the just-right gravity. The way you don't float off the floor, or feel like you've got a cannonball stuck to your head. People are hurrying past and round each other, with their bags and their strollers and their shopping carts. They come up to each other and then they go away and then they come back again. And it's all like a great big dance and everyone knows their moves. Then suddenly everyone—*everyone*—moves over toward the windows of Switched-On Electricals. As though some big comet with massive inherent gravity has gone by and they're all drawn to it. I can only see backs. People are standing on tiptoe. Dads are putting their kids on their shoulders. I know what they're doing. They're watching the launch of a rocket called the *Infinite Possibility*, which is going to send the first-ever child astronaut—a thirteen-year-old girl called Shenjian—into space. She's going to circumnavigate the moon. So she's not just going to be the first child in space; according to the TV, she's the first person to leave Earth's orbit since 1972. Everyone wants to see her. Her face is on the front of all the papers, on T-shirts, lunch boxes, mouse pads—anything you like.

One person has just left the crowd and is heading over to me. It's Dad. He's walking toward me like there's some special gravity pulling him toward me. And maybe there is. Maybe everyone's got their own special gravity that lets you go far away, really far away sometimes, but which always brings you back in the end. Because here's the thing. Gravity is variable. Sometimes you float like a feather. Sometimes you're too heavy to move. Sometimes one boy can weigh more than the whole universe. The universe goes on forever, but that doesn't make you small. Everyone is massive. Everyone is King Kong.

Dad says, "Aren't you coming to watch it?"

"Maybe later. I'm okay just now."

Everyone in the world remembers where they were when they heard about what Shenjian saw on the lunar surface.

I was standing in our kitchen. I was about to go to school. I'd just taken my end-of-term report out from under the little square gray stone that we use as a paperweight. Mom was reaching up to give me a kiss. "D'you know," she said, "I'm sure you've shrunk."

And she pushed me back against the "See How I Grow" chart and measured me. And it was true. I was half an inch shorter than I'd been the day I started at Waterloo High.

"Why doesn't that surprise me?" said Dad. "That would be typical Liam, wouldn't it? To start shrinking as he gets older. To spend his childhood six foot tall with a beard and his adulthood five foot nothing with a baby face."

The traffic update had just begun on the radio. Dad turned it up so he could hear properly when suddenly it stopped and the newsreader came on with this amazing report and went over live to the rocket. And Mom turned on the TV and I knew I wasn't going to school. No one was going anywhere that day.

Because Shenjian had found something on the moon.

"And really," said the announcer, "this find of hers changes everything. We've got pictures. Yes. There it is. There's no doubt about it. It's a man-made object. We know that no Apollo mission went to that part of the moon. It seems unlikely that a secret Russian or Chinese mission would leave a thing like this. . . . This is . . . extraordinary. Inexplicable. This changes our view of everything."

It was a load of rocks—squarish gray stones like the one on top of our kitchen cabinet. And all the stones were arranged to spell out some words. It couldn't be a coincidence because it was just so clear.

Florida rang up to make sure I was watching. "Remember the surprise?" she said.

I'd completely forgotten about it. But I saw it now. Spelled out across the lunar surface, two words—"Hello, Dad!"

I was grinning all over my face. I whispered, "Hello," into the phone. I was assuming that she'd written it for me. Now I come to think about it, maybe she was saying hello to the other dad, the one who'd left.

My dad looked across at me. He looked puzzled. Like he knew it had something to do with me. I said, "Hello, Dad." And he looked even more confused. When he hears this story maybe he'll think I got them to write it there for him. And maybe he'll be right. Maybe it was for both of us, and for other dads too. For all the dads on Earth. And for all the dads not on Earth. And for their dads, outward in space and backward in time, all the way to the Dad of the Universe.

And looking out into space, it sends a greeting from Earth to the Universe. Hello, Dad.

Acknowledgments

I can just about remember sitting on the couch with my parents, watching the first men land on the moon. We really did think that we were living in the space age and that by the time I had children we would all be able to go on space holidays together. Lots of other amazing things happened instead, of course, but I am still hoping that one day I'll go into space. In the meantime it seemed like it would be fun to go there in my own imagination. Of course, my own imagination couldn't generate the necessary escape velocity so I had to get help. I got it from:

Alan Bean—the fourth man to walk on the moon, and one of the most inspiring people on Earth—who very kindly let me use his name here; I also borrowed the name of the real Lorraine Sass, who made a generous donation to the Waterloo Partnership in exchange for appearing in this book. The Waterloo Partnership is helping to build a library and school in the real Waterloo in Sierra Leone. For more information see thewaterloopartnership.co.uk; Andrew

Smith's book *Moondust* never left my side while I was writing *Cosmic*; Danny Boyle first told me about Andrew's book and made an imaginary space journey of his own; Doug Millard of the Science Museum knows everything; all the information about World of Warcraft comes from my fine friend Sam Millar; Talya Baker made sure all the rivets on the rocket were nice and tight; the amazing Sarah Dudman stayed calm in Mission Control, even when I was rolling around in a very eccentric orbit; and Denise, my wife, had the courage to shoot me down in flames when I was flying off in the wrong direction.

EXPLORE MORE SPACE WITH NASA!

NASA and Space Center Houston want you to continue to explore space.

Play games, make discoveries, or simply join NASA in the journey to pioneer the future of space exploration, scientific discovery, and aeronautics research.

FOR FUN AND GAMES, VISIT THESE GREAT WEB PAGES

*** http://www.nasa.gov/audience/forkids/kidsclub/flash/index.html ***

This NASA website is especially for kids.

*** http://spaceyourface.nasa.gov/ ***

Show off your Moon Walk and learn about NASA's exciting plans for space exploration.

*** http://www.spacecenter.org/ ***

"Houston, we have visitors." Find out everything you need to visit NASA's Johnson Space Center in Houston, Texas.

FOLLOW NASA AT ALL YOUR FAVORITE PLACES

Twitter:	**http://twitter.com/NASA**
YouTube:	**http://www.youtube.com/user/ReelNASA**
Facebook:	**http://www.facebook.com/nasa.gov**
NASA Blogs:	**http://blogs.nasa.gov/cm/newui/blog/blogs.jsp**
Podcasts:	**http://www.nasa.gov/multimedia/podcasting/index.html**

FOR EDUCATORS

Professional Development

Visit Space Center Houston's website at

http://www.spacecenter.org for more information regarding:

Space Exploration Educator's Conference (SEEC)

Educator Open House

All Things NASA Can Be Found at

www.nasa.gov